Ordering Information:

Quantity sales. Special discounts are available on quantity purchases by corporations, associations, and others. For details, contact the publisher at the address above.

Please contact Author Daryl Omar @ 908-875-6799 and https://www.instagram.com/noveleden/ or through email at offredfc@gmail.com

Please leave a review on Goodreads, Amazon, Barnes & Noble, and BookBub!

Printed in the United States of America

Contents

Chapter One

I knew I would end up someone's villain after contemplating suicide. How I lived and why made me see that I would be the bad guy no matter what. I was living with my mother and fiancé.

My life felt like hell. One day, after months of dealing with my mother's heightened criticism and abuse, I decided I had to kill myself. I felt my purpose was in raising my son, but she thought I did nothing of value.

I thought if my mother doesn't like me then- well, what's it worth?

I wrote up the suicide letter. Beforehand, I tried talking to my fiancée—the two women, if not the only two people I wanted to love, always unrequited. I constantly felt like trash.

My choices were to either kill myself or leave. Since I am writing this, you may wonder how I am writing this while rotting in hell?

I prayed to the big guy, The Highest God of the Universe and Multiverse, mindful of how he felt about suicide. We had a long talk about how I felt about his son. When our conversation, I awoke in the middle of the road and was hit by a bus. I died instantly and didn't remember any real pain.

I spent a while in purgatory. Long enough, anyone who would have missed me had moved on or forgotten about me. And my feelings about being dead could finally settle. So many spirits stalk around the mortal realm, envious of the material and living. We were all classified as "wanton wastes of potential." With a label like that, it was no surprise many caused trouble or haunted the mortals.

The processing for purgatory is arduous. It felt like a brand-new lifetime—a life of contemplation, reflection, and meditation. Purgatory is vacuous. The parts that aren't overly bureaucratic like spending a lifetime in the DMV or an open void. Those who repent in purgatory time are reassigned and bypassed into heaven. But, at the same time, those who cause havoc even in their time of reflection get condemned to hell. The problem is getting those spirits to hell after they leave purgatory.

The day I left Purgatory, Jesus was waiting for me with St. Peter. He pulled me aside from the long line into heaven to offer me the opportunity in his suicide prevention unit.

I serve as a guardian angel for at-risk boys in the suicide prevention unit. I thought I would be in the call-center answering prayers. Considering suicide is the third leading killer of men, I am far too busy to have an office job. There were perks to spending more time on the pale blue dot. At least I wasn't in hell. But, whenever needed, I get immediately absorbed into the land of mortals.

It's happening again! I don't even have a body, which still makes me hurl.

A portal of purple energy opens up, sucking me inside. The portal spits me out onto a vermillion orange bridge, where I see a young man around five foot five on the bridge wearing a black hoodie. A dark cloud loomed over his head.

I can see him in my ephemeral state, but he can't see me. I shook off trans-dimensional travel while he liked most of the boys I find at the bridges. My new friend was staring over the edge, in awe of the distance he may fall. Most walked away if they cared about pain, but he shut his eyes, refusing to look any longer, clenching the bridge.

"Come on. I can't chicken out now."

"It's not quite chickening out if it's a bad idea. More of a reconsideration." I materialized directly next to him. Impossible to be a passerby or a stopped car.

"What, what? Who are you?" he cried out, falling over his feet.

"I'm Carter. God sent me because he thought you planned to hop over that bridge." So I stared down, whistling at the distance.

"There is no God."

"Now, you see why you're suicidal." I sigh.

"This some joke to you?" he says defensively.

"I'm not laughing, pal. Death is a grave matter. I gave you my name. What's yours?" I turned my body square to his hunched-over the frame as he looked at the San Francisco Bay below.

"Why does it matter? I'm going to die soon anyway."

"You don't have to die. So why do you have to die?"

"I have nothing back home. I just got into a fight with my mom, and she kicked me out of the house because I was overreacting. I have nowhere to go now!" he cried.

"And you think if your mom doesn't love you, then no one will love you?" So I asked with empathy in my tone.

"Well, the kids at school already bullied me. My dad moved out a couple of years ago. My mom got me Into the courts. All she does now is go on dates, party, and spend my dad's check. So I ask her about camps, sports, or college, then she curses me out, saying I'm just like my dad."

"That sounds painful, my friend."

"One of my friends at school showed me my mom's Only Fans account today, and when I asked her about it, I got kicked out. She said I could leave if I didn't like how she made her money. So, I left."

"I feel your pain, I truly do, but I can't imagine how you feel."

"I feel like a piece of shit. I'm only a freshman, and every guy at school has seen my mom naked doing all types of things on camera! They even try to sleep with her for money! I just- I just want to die, man. I can't ever go back to school or be at home."

"Well, do you want to die, or do you want a different life?"

He wiped his tears away, pondering my question for a few seconds before opening his mouth as though it had never been an option.

"I guess I want it all to be different." He sniffles.

"Where is dad?"

"He moved to Oakland in some gated community."

"It sounds weird you don't get to see him. I mean, you're only in San Francisco."

"My mom doesn't let him visit. She told the courts she only wanted the money. She put a restraining order against him because he spanked me. I haven't seen him since he left."

"Would you rather live with your dad?"

His tears dried as he gave a short decisive nod. His chest was rising and falling with anticipation as he watched me maul over how I would pull this off.

As a Guardian Angel, I only have enough money to buy the kid a dinner or an ice cream cone if there are too many attempts in one day. So it's nice to enjoy real food again, even if it's only the taste. Hopefully, Christ will understand me going a bit away from training to solve this case. Of course, the best things in life didn't require any money, and they only took an effort to achieve anything beneficial.

"I can take you to your dad." I convinced myself despite never being the best at flying.

"What, really!?" he cheered.

"Do you think it'll be different living with him?"

"All my mom does anymore is hurt my feelings or argue with me over any and everything. She treats me like she treated my dad. I want to leave Carter. I have to leave."

"Let's go, to Oakland it is, and that would be, uh help me out buddy where is Oakland, that north, my north westish? Alright, I'm not a good flyer, and I'm from heaven, nowhere like California, so you're going to have to give me directions."

"It's literally across the bridge."

"Wow, he's been that close all this time?"

"I know..." he sulked.

I spread my wings, hovering above the ground. I held out a hand, hoping the kid would come. He takes another look over the bridge. He pries his hands off the railing, tiptoeing closer to me.

"Please don't drop me, Carter."

"What's your name, kid?"

"Pablo, Pablo Rivera." He grabs my hand.

"A strong name for a powerful boy."

"I don't feel strong."

"You had to be strong for too long. Now, you are exhausted. The weight of your cross has drained you. It doesn't take away from how long you've been carrying that yok. It's good you finally dropped the cross because it wasn't yours to carry."

"Whoa..."

"It's the truth," I assured.

We had flown over the bridge. I began looking down at the lit cities and dead zones. It felt like many of California were hills, woods, and forests with pockets of people gathered about or living independently. It didn't help I was nearsighted, struggling to tell the different areas apart. It looked the same, divided by pride, perspective, and delusion.

I couldn't tell Oakland was distinctly different from its surrounding area if you paid me from this far away. It didn't matter. All I wanted was for this boy to avoid my fate. If I could manage that, then I could be joyful. To know he would be good with his Pops was enough for me.

"They're that's his apartment complex!" Pablo screams.

"Great, a complex how will you know which apartment is his with all these units?" I felt my wings pulling against the air friction as I lowered from the high altitude. I tugged against the air feeling like a second pair of arms in a moving car as we began coasting for the ground in a free fall to save me the strain.

"Are we crashing?" Pablo panicked while squeezing me tighter.

"Basically."

I smirked, remembering my lessons from Guardian Angel training. Okay, tuck in your wings and barrel roll. Now open your wings and decelerate, then glide. Okay, much smoother now.

"Whoa, you are a terrible flier." Pablo jumped to the ground.

He was puking, falling over his side, staring at the red concrete. He hugged the manicured grass beneath his face, washing away his puke with a half-drunken water bottle littered on the ground. He kissed the clean grass as tears swelled in his eyes.

"Hey, I'm not that bad of a flier that you have to cry and whatnot."

"No, I'm so happy to be alive! Thank you, thank you so much, Carter. I didn't want to die." Pablo sobbed as I patted his back.

"Hey, hey, relax, bud. It's not your fault for not wanting to live in your situation. You didn't ask for it, never wanted it, and walked away. Your mom selfishly created her living hell. You were her last slice of heaven. Now, she's lost it and must navigate the world alone." I recited what Jesus had said after the bus hit me, and he walked with me through the void into limbo.

I felt the dark cloud returning as if materializing known too far away. It felt more potent than at the bridge.

"Pablo, go to the front office. Let them know you're looking for your dad. Have him pick you up. Call the police at the main office and inform them of everything that's happened. Get a lawyer. Hell will rise against you, but victory is in the name of Christ our Lord and Savior." I pat his shoulder.

"Will I ever see you again?" Pablo asked.

"Hopefully, when it's your time, but not sooner. I tried to take my own life, and I wish I had just moved in with my dad. Now run along because my job is starting soon. God bless you, Pablo. May Jesus protect you!" So I hurried him on his way.

I felt the energy change in the air entirely as Pablo left. An older man stood behind us, and his eyes followed Pablo. Then his body began gently walking past me. His energy made my wings quiver. The octagenarian hissed, cursing under his breath and muttering to himself as he began walking past me.

I left the material world, reentering the spiritual plane, and as I suspected, a sullen 8ft tall lust demon possessed the body. An incubus spirit haunting the monster was not far from the demon's side.

"Hello, gentlemen." I greet.

"Oh shit, you can see us?" the incubus spirit spoke in a rushed tone.

"Hmph... an angel, this turned into a bad day." The lust demon grumbled, rubbing its rotund belly.

"You wouldn't be interested in my young friend, gentlemen?" So I cautiously approached, remaining out of arm's reach.

The spirit spits, buzzing around my head in its wisp form, "Do you have jurisdiction here, little birdie?"

"They call me Carter, Guardian Angel Department of Heaven. Detective first class. Do you gentlemen have your papers?"

"Yeah, I got them." The lust demon offered willingly, wanting to rush me off.

"A standard demonic possession, I see. And a lifelong atheist. I see you have your rites in order. I'm not here to give you gentlemen a hard time. However, I am asking about your friend, not you." So I turn my attention to the wisp, looking it dead in its microscopic eyes.

The demon rushed away. The disabled older man dropped his walker and began sprinting away faster than Usain Bolt.

"You're under arrest under the jurisdiction of Heaven and Yeshua Hamashiach, The Christ." I bark.

"Ha, you know you done fucked up, right?" the incubus spirit's voice turned into a husky, graveled guttural grumble as he laughed. Materializing into the spiritual plane as a 15ft blob of pus, ectoplasm, and gray matter.

I had a good hunch this wouldn't end so easy. It rarely ever does when spirits get involved. Demons typically wanted to find their way to heaven eventually. Damned souls wanted to take as many people with them to hell as possible. So getting them off the Earth to hell wasn't an enviable task.

"I don't want to have to kill you. I am a detective. I want to know why so many men have been attempting to commit suicide. I want to know why I find so many demons haunting the earth. Why are there so many Damned Spirits?"

"Do you think I want some little birdie pecking in my business?" he lashed out with two tentacles, grasping my arms and dragging me to its beaked mouth.

"Are you the boss?" I continue my interrogation.

"You're asking a lot of questions. I was going to eat you. I think I'm going to rape my first birdie."

"Oh, eating me was your trump card? I thought it was your only card." I say, opening my hand to summon my sword of the spirit. So I twisted my wrist, slicing off his tentacles at light speed.

"Damn you!" he cried out in pain.

"Now, will you answer my questions?" I asked, sheathing my blade.

"You bastard! I won't let you get to the boss!"

"You didn't strike me as leadership material. What is your boss' participation in the suicide epidemic?"

"Fuck you!"

"You're leaving me little choice," I say, rolling out the way to avoid his grasp.

I pray, "Full armor of God, protect me from all evil and dark spirits!"

A heavenly ray of light shines down from the night sky. I am enveloped in heaven's rays as my belt of truth, the breastplate of righteousness, grieves of peace, the shield of faith, and helmet of salvation absorbed the strike on my guard. I was shaking him off as if using an umbrella for the gentle breeze. Invoked with the power of God, I charged in, slicing my sword once, twice, one hundred times, sending ethereal waves of light through the incubus spirit. Each wave detonated on contact until nothing was left but a beak attached to gray matter.

"You tried to kill me! Thou shalt not kill. You're not an angel!" the incubus spirit fumed.

"I am under orders by Yeshua Hamashiach, The Christ. He has sent me to investigate. My glory and my sins forgiven, I am repentant. Turn yourself over to Christ. Help me, join us under the cross."

"You killed me!"

"Embrace Christ!"

"He'll eviscerate my spirit. I already can't return to the physical world for my sins. And you have destroyed my ephemeral body!"

"Would you rather return to hell than ever experience heaven?"

"Jesus would never let me into heaven."

"Repent, repent now and give me a lead. If you help me, then I can help you! I can arrest you back to purgatory instead of killing you!"

"Jezebel wants to kill all the men. All the men with strong spirits must be broken emotionally or removed physically were her orders." His beak cawed.

"Why?"

"Ask her. I'm just doing my job."

"You have a demon underneath you as a spirit. You're choosing what you want to tell me. I need a lead! Tell me what I need to know to end this, not what saves your ass for one more year!" I demanded, stabbing my blade through the gray matter.

The incubus spirit cries in agony, "Alright, alright… she is creating an army on Earth. She's making a play, and Jezebel has overthrown Satan."

"How did you manage that at all?"

"With Lilith and Ahab."

"Damn… how big is this army?"

The incubus spirit began laughing, "One million strong and counting. You'll never stop her because you're already too late. Might I mention one million demons born on Earth that she has raised for decades? You have no idea how many humans we have supporting our vision of spiritual domination."

"What 8 billion humans?" I scoffed at his bluff.

"You're smug now. I failed but wait until Ahab or Lilith get their hands on you. Now, arrest me and take me to heaven!"

"Your spirits are all so ignorant. All you did was confess by telling on other people. Your act isn't repentance. It isn't turning against your evil and opening your heart to virtue. Know we just met, but I truly wished I could have saved your eternal soul."

I prepare my prison prism to teleport him to the purgatory prison units.

"No, no, I don't want to be anything!" he cried.

"Repent… or I have no choice but to be sent to purgatory prison for eternity." So I finished my prism, beginning to cast it around him.

"Ha, you know what, pretty boy? You talk too much. You're about to meet all my friends." The beak began laughing hysterically with malice in his guffaws.

His reinforcements surrounded me. A dozen demons stood against me, snarling, holding their weapons.

"Do you know the difference between an angel and a demon? I believe you'll soon realize. Satan himself could stand before me, and you will still need reinforcements. Father God, lend me your strength. I accept you are within me, and I am here for your will to be done. God, your will be done, thy kingdom comes, as Earth as it is in heaven."

The night sky parted. I turned my back, walking away as a ray of divine light fell from the sky, wiping the demons from existence. I must find a way back to heaven. I just missed my ride. I have 24hrs until I can call another strike like that one. While I'm stuck on Earth, I guess I could figure out how to stop Jezebel, Lilith, and Ahab from destroying Earth.

Where are the true believers? I need reinforcements if I am going to fight against millions of demons. After seeing that strike, fighting against every demon in California will be on me. That was already a lot before finding out about Jezebel's plot.

I turned, seeing the-wisp floating above my head, having avoided the strike entirely, "Hey Carter, you bastard. Now, you'll learn the difference between a spirit and an angel!" he bellowed, moving five times faster than I could track with my eyes.

I looked on to see him releasing his toxic demon spores from its body, infecting all the humans out and about. Corrupting their souls on contact, twisting their souls from their bodies, creating more demons from their vessels as their weak spirits turned into 6-foot and 10-foot nightmares searching the streets for me.

"God, have I failed you?" I pleaded for answers as I fell to my knees in tears looking at the mess I had created.

Chapter Two

In the path of the Incubus spirit, all the humans outdoors were infected with spores. Without a tidal wave of holy water, there was no way left to fight but prayer.

"Father God, I have failed you. I cannot do this alone." I look up to the sky in tears.

"Are you done crying, or do you need a hug?" a frail man rocking dreadlocks kneeled by my side, offering his hand.

"I could use a hug." I sniffle, standing up.

"Self-pity attracts more demons and dark spirits. Are you alright, Carter?"

How does he know my name? His energy felt so pure. Simply standing close to him, I felt my energy and confidence return. He wore an emerald-green sweater and rose-red jeans. I couldn't wrap my brain around where I knew him, but I knew him. He led the way tugging me along as we ran to avoid the humans who began giving birth to demons. Then, filling their vessels, we ran for higher ground, leaving the streets filled with hundreds of monsters. Each second passing, more demons were born from the spores leaving battered bodies on the floor from the exhaustion of birth. So it took only minutes for the monsters to grow full-size.

"I've never seen a full-fledge demon invasion. I can't imagine how you plan to fight all those demons." My new friend watched from the fire escape.

"I prayed for help. I need a warrior to help me, no offense." So I sighed, sitting on the rooftop, looking at my mess.

"I am the help. Yeshua sent you a cleric. You are the warrior, Carter. You seriously need more confidence. If you can't master that, then have faith in God." He pats my back.

"If we touch that pavement, we will get swarmed and sent back to heaven." My heartfelt heavy.

"Not if we're wise. We need some cover. There has to be a church or mosque nearby." He suggests.

"I believe I passed a few religious buildings when I was flying here. You know my name, but who do I thank for lifting my spirits?" I extend my arm.

"I am Archangel Raphael."

"You are thee, Raphael? You- you're a member of the Sefirot! You're one of the top ten strongest angels!"

"Oh, stop!" Raphael gleams with a proud smile.

"I had no idea, and I'm so sorry for insulting you!"

"Oh, okay, it's okay!" Raphael laughs.

"Wow… but- if Yeshua sent an Archangel, he believes this is pretty serious."

"Jesus sent you because he thought it was severe!" Raphael mentions.

I wiped my eyes, realizing his truth, accepting my reality. I'm who Jesus sent to fix this problem? Wow, he must believe in me. And I can't even believe in myself. I have to get up before all of California is infected if I'm all that's coming. So we need to move quickly."

In his physical form, Raphael had no wings. However, his powerful aura was like a bright light for flies. He had something more profound than confidence causing the demons to shift to attacking the building. He had the utmost faith in Yeshua and Yahweh. Then, simply being around Raphael, I felt my spirit rise and strength return as if we handled this situation even if I had no idea how to fix it.

"About a mile south, there's a Church of Latter-Day Saints."

"Not my first pick, but it's a house of God." Raphael quips.

"3 miles away is a Mosque." I shrug.

"Oh, so much better but too far. The demons or their scouts will spot us if we're out too long. I heard from Michael and Zadkiel that you haven't adjusted to having wings. So I guess we go to the Mormons."

"Great, even Michael knows I suck at flying. Zadkiel trained me, so I'm not too surprised he knew." My cheeks turned red, thinking the strongest of all Archangels knew I was a bad flier.

I grabbed Raphael, and we set out for the skies. Below us were thousands of demons without sight of the Incubus Spirit that caused all this havoc. In his wisp form, he'll be nearly impossible to find. He likely released his spores and then got even smaller in size. Regardless, it wouldn't matter. I would need to find Lilith or Ahab. I knew Ahab had moved into Hollywood, but I had no idea where Lilith would be considering everything going on.

Chapter Three

Arriving at the Oakland California Temple of Latter-Day Saints felt like coming to the Taj Mahal. A beautiful ivory building, glowing ominously orange-yellow in the night sky with shining gold pyramids crowing the building.

Raphael whistled as we landed at the front door. A series of demons were banging against the force field protecting the building. We were safe for now. If the barrier remained, we would be able to rest until sunrise.

I knocked on the front door, hearing the knock echo throughout the building before a young woman arrived at the door.

"Um, hello, we are in a bible study with recruits. How can I help you?" A beautiful dark-skinned woman answered, stepping outside wearing a warm smile as if she couldn't see the thousands of demons banging against the force field.

"Um, hello, Miss," I say, stunned I even found humans attractive.

Raphael chuckled to himself, noticing my nervousness.

"We needed refuge for the night." I bowed my head, closing my wings.

"I'm not sure if we have any space available. We have more missionaries here than usual. And Heavenly Father has blessed us with many souls seeking to spread his word." She cheers joyously.

"Uh, ha, that's awesome." I smiled hazily.

"My friend and I only need a few hours to rest. We are on assignment from The Heavenly Father. The rest of the area is quite sinful, and we wanted to sit in a temple to pray." Raphael spoke for us.

"Of course! If you would like to pray, we are always open. Honesty, you may take a nap in the pews. Elder Price and Deacon Young are present if you want someone to pray with tonight." She offers.

"Thank you for your kindness, ma'am." So I bow my head out of respect.

"Sister Davies and you?" she gleamed, extending her hand to me.

"Enoch... Carter." I mumble, taking her hand and kissing her knuckles.

Sister Davies blushed, letting us inside the temple. Raphael nudged me with his elbow, giving me a wink.

"So, Enoch, are you a believer?" she follows closely by my side.

"I work for Jesus," I admit.

"Oh? We hear that often. Sometimes people deceive themselves when they haven't met Heavenly Father. Perhaps, you would like to have a bible study session with me?" she offers.

Raphael begins snickering, "You two seem to be smitten at first sight."

I blushed, being caught out. I hoped my feelings for humans had fled me, but her spirit was so powerful. She felt divine. I was captivated by her beauty and devotion to tending the temple late at night while most others were asleep or possessed by demons.

"We are on official business Carter." Raphael reminds me politely.

"Could I possibly help?" Sister Davies insists.

"I think it might help Carter more if you gave us some space," Raphael suggests.

"Oh well, I understand." She frowns for a moment, then her eyes light up again, "You are a good friend for keeping your friend chaste. My sister missionary advises I avoid being alone with men as well. If you both want to join our bible study, please join us in room 2."

"Thank you dearly." I smile, blushing if I'm honest.

Raphael let out a sigh waiting until she left us before he spoke. "Lust inside a temple?"

"It isn't lusting, and her spirit is stronger than any mortals I've ever felt. Are you sure she's human?" I asked.

"I felt her power too. She's a true child of God. And that is something you nor any man should defile. If she has a strong spirit, then leave her for God. We are only here to rest, and then we must deal with those demons. If you do anything for a mortal, feel the need to protect them from evil."

"Where were girls like her when I was alive?"

"In church, where were you?"

"Touché." I sighed, letting go of the fantasy as she entered the parish hall with long pews, with a sanitized energy all over the room. It felt more like a movie set than a church. "I can still hear the demons clawing at the barrier."

"We need to evacuate the temple," Raphael notes.

"Why?" I asked.

Raphael points to a black wisp floating around the pulpit. A dark spirit had entered the church while demons were barred. Spirits moved freely. It was looking for a way to drop the barrier, I reckon. I quietly sat down, bowing my head and preparing a prism for the dark spirit. Raphael walked around, keeping the spirit's attention like a fly attracted to light. We only had one attempt to protect the temple.

"Purgatory Prison!" I teleported the prism, entrapping the spirit, trying wildly to escape it, "Banishment!"

"Great job!" Raphael announces.

"Wow..." Sister Davies mused from far away.

The dark spirit was eliminated from the physical world. We could have avoided this ordeal if I had moved quickly against the Incubus Spirit. Raphael and I both turned our attention to Sister Davies and a dower older man by her side.

"Witchcraft in a temple of God?" he curses at us, marching down the aisle.

"It wasn't witchcraft. It's divine magic." Raphael retorted.

"There is no divine magic, all magick is evil and an act against *Gawd* Almighty!" the old man continues with timbre in his speech.

"This is why we should have gone to the mosque. The Muslims have been slaying demons for centuries. They would say thank you for banishing dark spirits. So my question is, why is there a dark spirit inside your temple?" Raphael confronts him.

"I- I have no idea." Deacon Young calmed down.

"I am Carter, and this is Raphael. We are servants of Jesus the Christ."

The old man nodded, "I appreciate your manners, young man."

"Sister Davies said you had a couple of people in Bible Study. Are they your usuals?" I asked.

"No, two strange young folks. A boy and a girl seemed hungrier for food and shelter than the word of God. So we are fixing a small dinner if you would care to join us." Sister Davies invites.

"Mind your place!" the old man snaps at her.

"Apologies, Elder Young."

"May we join your bible study?" I suggest.

"Yes!" Sister Davies cheers.

"Hmm... you seem hungry for something different than food or God, young man. Sister Davies is a missionary. She is here to grow in her relationship with God, not with strange boys. Unless, of course, you wish for a baptism." Elder Young cut straight to the point.

"I am not allowed to date either." I bow my head.

"Perfect." Elder Young pats my shoulders, "Who are you, boy? My student here tells me much about you but very little of substance."

"My mother named me Enoch, sir."

"Hm... I have had time to read and understand the missing sections of the bible in my seminary years. Understanding how much was removed from the Bible made Joseph's Smith New Testament compelling. Where the old church had fallen apart, divided us, and was at war amongst itself. Smith created a new church, thriving in this modern era of sin and iniquity." Elder Young's grip tightened on my shoulder.

"I thank you for your perspective. When you put it that way, it makes more sense why so many Believers found their home in Mormonism." I say, politely shrugging off his grip, stepping to Raphael's side.

"Mormon was a man. The man who wrote our sacred texts. An indigenous man, a military leader over the people who came before Columbus. Mormon was a warrior who fought bravely for years before submitting himself to God. Even in the Godless Americas, as the Sisters Taught me as a boy, God found a mouthpiece. He created this Temple. We are simply moving hands allowing him to do his works on Earth, or we prevent his works from being done. I have followed God into Catholic Seminary, and I followed God away from Catholicism to join this church of Saints in the End times. I will not stand in your way, but I must know the truth, Brother Enoch." Elder Young spoke so sharply and articulate, clear as a Buddhist chanting bowl, almost musical yet poise and pious.

"You have a gift for speeches Father Young. My compatriot and I are tasked by Jesus the Christ and the Highest God to investigate a series of suicides. We are Angels of the Guardian Angel Bureau in heaven. We came seeking refuge, but we believe your divine barrier has already been penetrated."

"Holy Shit." Elder Young holds his chest as I release my wings to confirm what I'm saying.

"Then it is true. My vision is coming true." So Sister Davies frowned, holding her chest and suddenly falling to her knees in exasperation.

"I cannot believe my eyes, ears, or mind. It is true. God, God is real." Elder Young stammered in disbelief.

"Well, of course, he's real. I forgot most pastors are Atheists these days." Raphael quips.

"This isn't merely a set of codes and rules to live your life. It is the pathway on how to live, as I learned the hard way. Can you tell you about your vision, sister?"

"I- I fear it may not help. A few nights ago, I had a dream of encountering two demons in the flesh. I would do all I could to compel their hearts to God. And then a woman came, a blonde-haired woman with crystalline teal eyes and skin pale as porcelain. When she touched me, I felt things I had never felt before lust, rage, pain. And then, when she pulled her hand away, I felt nothing. Then she grew angry. I was wearing a white smock, and she wore a black one but dirtied as if it had once been white. She did all she could, chasing me with paint, ink, and mud, trying to dirty me. But I awoke suddenly, and she was gone. Today, I found these two teens who looked homeless, and all afternoon, it's been arguments and outrage over God. We have fed them, offered them refuge, and still they do nothing but haze me and insult my church. Then you came."

"The woman. Did she have wings like a bat and a glare that could turn your heart ice cold?" Raphael asked.

"Yes." Sister Davies said, amazed.

"Lilith." Raphael attested ruefully, holding his hand over his heart.

"Did we walk into her trap?" I asked, shocked.

"The League of Satan had long infiltrated the church. Jesus told me of the evils of the church in his day. The church that once crucified Jesus had been killed, and the church remained. Christ's death divided the Synagogue of Satan and The Church of Christ. Before, these devils could move through the church as true believers. However, those who refused Christ became clear. The war had always been, but his death created clear battle lines between good and evil. Those who refuse Christ as savior and redeemer are condemned to hell. There is nothing to be done to save their soul. They are the descendants of those who murdered Christ. Until they repent for the sins of their ancestors, then nothing can be done for them." Elder Young explained again, "This is why I left Catholicism. To see the sins of man and do nothing but condemn and judge. I knew there was a solution. A way to help humanity, I knew it was in the Bible, but Joseph Smith showed me how to unlock its potential."

"Patrick Henry Young, are you of the Church of Christ?" Raphael stood before me and Sister Davies.

The Elderly Father's face became paler as he smiled at us, his skin peeled away as if it were fake. As though something had been living in his skin for quite some time. Deacon Young's body fell to the floor as his skin bulged in certain places. Something inside was trying to get out.

"Prepare your Prism, Carter!" Raphael shouts as he leaps to Deacon Young's body, holding his mouth shut.

"Purgatory Prism." I extended my hands as the geometrical pattern began to form.

"Ready?"

"Yes!" I shout.

He opens Elder Young's mouth as a Pride Demon crawls out his flesh, leaving the Deacon's body like a squeezed tube of toothpaste. I cast my prism, the shape encapsulating the 10ft demon's taking up the entire room. In moments he was gone, banished back to hell after judgment. The Elder's body bled, his bones broken, tears streaming down his eyes as he chanted, "It's real, God is real." In a state of shock.

"What is going on!" Sister Davies demands.

"Looks like a wisp has possessed this guy." I tried to sound professional but felt so awkward with a man bleeding to death on the floor.

"A wisp? Should we call 911?"

"If we call an ambulance, we have no idea what could be coming through on the truck. I can heal The Deacon. Carter, do you think you can take on those two demons yourself?" Raphael asked.

I looked at the despair and exhaustion in Sister Davies' face, and her energy was almost entirely depleted from only meeting her. I nodded, convinced I needed to protect this girl. I drew my sword, heading for the girl.

"Wait, the girl. Watch out for the girl." Sister Davies recommends.

"Why?"

"I think she's the same girl from my vision."

Raphael went cold, "here?"

"And you wanted to go to the mosque."

"We walked into her trap."

"A mosque was recently burned down in Oakland. When it was reported on the news during dinner, she laughed as if she had started the fire. I felt nothing but pure evil in her soul." Sister Davies explains.

"I will join you, Carter. We can go together if you want to wait for me to finish healing the Elder."

"I need to fix my mess." I nodded in confirmation, pushing the door open and charging forward for door number two.

As I got down the hallway, the temperature dropped, freezing every breath I took. So I reached for the door, unready for what awaited on the other side.

The entire children's bible study room was covered in blood as a woman sat alone in the middle of the room naked as the day she was born with bat's wings spread wide. Her eyes could have turned my stone as we made eye contact. I stood in the doorway clenching my blade, noticing the clothes of the young boy torn apart under her bare, blistered feet with claws rather than nails growing from her feet.

"You are all they sent?" she asked innocently.

"Aye." I nodded, not wanting to give away Raphael's presence.

"Fun." She stands beginning to approach me, standing at six-foot-tall, peering down at me as she comes to the door.

I raised my blade, shifting my body back to keep her at bay.

"If you could cut off my head, you would have done so already. Instead, you study me as if you are witnessing a sculpture at the museum."

"I'm looking at you like I'm on the other side of a bulletproof window at the looney bin. You killed this kid?"

"We got a bit bored waiting. This boy's idea of fun was fondling my breasts. And well, this was mine." She giggles.

I grit my teeth, growling, "Why are you here?"

"I got word someone was interfering with my plans. Who knew trusting so many demons and dictators would have gone awry? So, I came seeking salvation. Instead, I found you." Lilith reached for me, and I sliced the air making her step back, hissing at me.

"You brought your entire army to find salvation?"

"Oh no, this isn't my entire army. I heard there was a reformed demon doing work here. I sought wisdom to get right with God before he comes back."

"He?"

"Oh, come on, Detective. You know who he is. Doesn't he give you all goosebumps?"

"The Devil is already a defeated foe, Lilith, as are you." I point my sword to her throat, and she backs up, cutting her eyes.

"I sincerely think you lack the cruelty to kill someone so reasonable and beautiful as myself. I was enough to get Adam to forsake his vows. He was the first man. Do you think you match up?" she licked the tip of my sword.

"So, I'm not killing you. You're not killing me. What's the point?" I ask.

“So, you admit Adam is better than you?”

“I never met him. I only care about Jesus’ perspective of me.”

“Isn’t that demeaning?”

“The world is judging demeaning. You are under arrest Lilith.”

“That’s fine, and then you can clean up the demons yourself as they riot for their new Queen.”

“You think you overthrew Satan?”

“Worse, I ratted him out. He was an Angel like you, it makes people think he quit working for his dad, but he’s on God’s payroll. He tricked me long ago. He tricked Adam and his new playmate. So, I got him back. We don’t trust Angels in hell. So, why trust Satan? He’s doing his best to hold back my forces. A hundred thousand years of damned, evil, demented, and maladjusted souls following a lowly Angel with daddy issues? So, I bossed up and did what was necessary. Now, I’m running the show. Satan is daddy’s little girl, and you, my friend, are under arrest.” Lilith's smile turned her back to me entirely.

"Our Queen, are you hurt?" two boys wearing black pants and white shirts ran up to us.

I thought this building was empty. Lilith already infected the others in here. So, maybe Elder Young did have our best interest at heart.

"Did you two find the source of the barrier, as I asked?" Lilith looks over the long sharp nails.

"Who is this guy? Is he bothering you, Mistress?" the larger one of the two pokes me in the chest.

"You're trying to drop the barrier?" So I stepped back, only finding the wall behind me.

"It should be dropped if these two idiots were useless. I asked if you found the barrier. Never mind who he is. Pay attention to your new Queen of the Universe!" Lilith demands in a gnarled deep demonic voice rumbling the room.

"Yes, Mistress!" The boys cry in unison out of fear.

"Yes, you found the barrier?"

"No... we don't know what barriers are, and we can't find Elder Young."

"Young was supposed to meet us here to finish the angel."

"I already banished him back to Purgatory." I raised my hands, already holding up my prism, "You'll see him soon."

Lilith's eyes widen before turning into liquid, dropping into a pool of blood evading the prism.

"Jonah, Thomas, run away!" Sister Davies shouts from up the hall.

The two boys returned to their senses, stumbling over themselves and running for Sister Davies.

Lilith appeared between them. "Sorry boys, I'm going to need a bit more people juice to drop barrier the old-fashioned way. Your incompetence has forced me to go nuclear."

"We are all responsible for our actions." Sister Davies shouts.

"Oh, shut your trap. Poor naïve little sheep following after a wolf disguised as a shepherd."

"Even wolves can be shepherds, as dogs learned over the centuries. You could have changed. You choose bitterness. Let my friends go from your evil spell!" Sister Davies demands.

"You know what. I think one of you will be enough. You." Lilith darts for Sister Davies, who shrieks.

I ram all my force into the boys, toppling them like dominos and leaping over them. Then, as I brought my blade down, Lilith once more turned herself to blood and pooled away.

"Dammit." Lilith curses.

"Your pride has got the best of you!" Sister Davies cheered from behind me.

"Don't you ever shut up?" Lilith fumes.

"Purgatory Prism!" I release another while she is distracted with Sister Davies.

Lilith smiles as tendrils of blood grow from her back, grasping Jonah and Thomas. She tossed one of the boys into the prism and the other onto me. Before she darts for Sister Davies, grabbing her by the neck, a tendril slowly rises to Sister Davies' cheeks, and Lilith gleamed at the horror in Sister Davies's eyes.

"Heavenly Father, please protect me in my time of need." Sister Davies utters.

I roar, tossing the two-hundred-pound boy off me as if it were a blanket. I release my sword, manifesting a mace to batter through her hardened blood tendrils as she inched away, carrying Sister Davies. Lilith smugly smiled, unable to see Raphael behind her. As quiet as a church mouse, Raphael summoned a staff and swiped Sister Davies from Lilith's hands in one swing, bashing the butt of the staff's flesh against Lilith's skull in the second movement.

Lilith raised a ball of blood around her shielding herself from our attacks.

"Now, Carter!" Raphael barks.

"Purgatory Prism!" I call out.

"So predictable." Lilith dispersed the ball of blood, nowhere to be found, and neither was Sister Davies.

"No! No! No! We had her dead to rites!"

"Yes, you did. Why didn't you attack Lilith sooner? We could have gotten the mortals out of processing in purgatory." Raphael slaps his forehead.

"I… I could reason with Lilith."

"You tried to reason with an evil spirit? I wasn't expecting her to be right under our nose. She's toying with us."

"And she took Sister Davies!"

Raphael rubbed his temples, "I should have come with you. The Deacon's body was a husk, and the demon became a priest of his own volition."

"Many take up that path. Reformed Demons that had fallen to Satan, so they have worn a mortal for a suit for redemption. Lilith brings them straight down to hell with her. What is she doing on earth if she fights a war in hell?"

"Thinking like a detective, we must have had her closed off if she took a hostage."

"Lilith said something about making things right with God before Satan returns. So, she must have fled hell. The wisps must be rounding up all the demons on earth, creating more."

"She's attempting to start the apocalypse." Raphael covered his mouth.

"What?"

"If the earth gets overrun with demons again, as it did with the fallen angels, God will have to purge them. There would be no way to purge a demon invasion on earth without killing every human. The threat of the demons would be too great. God could always create new humanity or new earth, but demons are trans-dimensional. Once they overrun the earth, they could overtake other planets or parallel universes. The only option would be using the apocalypse." Raphael wore a solemn expression holding back a sea of tears.

"My failure caused the apocalypse."

"We haven't failed yet. We're in this together. We know Lilith couldn't have left the building yet. The alarm system hasn't gone off."

"Unless she went through the ephemeral plane?"

"Do you think she killed Sister Davies?" Raphael sobbed.

I showed him the room I found Lilith in.

"I see why you couldn't move. To believe something can be so evil yet so convicted in its selfish motives. Samael was a jerk, but he was conflicted over his evil. This

Lilith is a different level of a cruelty altogether. She is nothing like us."

"Maybe she's nothing like you, but as long as she has Sister Davies, I'm willing to do whatever it takes to get her back."

"Carter. Let the mortal go." Raphael stares me dead in the eyes.

I choked back tears.

"You are falling into Lilith's trap. She's in your head, man. She's using Sister Davies against you." Raphael taps my skull.

"No, you just don't care about her because she's just some lowly mortal to you!" I swat his hand away.

"Carter, she is setting you against me! She knows your power and is trying to use you against Jesus' purpose for you. Listen to me! You have to let Sister Davies go!" Raphael tried to reason.

I felt torn between my former humanity and my divinity. My heart was breaking as I released the depths of my failures. I banished an innocent boy and caused a poor girl her death because I couldn't take down Lilith.

"Carter, you need to get it together, man. If we find Lilith, we can bring an end to this, and if the girl is still alive, then great. For now, we need to focus on stopping Lilith and nothing else. We couldn't have stopped those mortals from dying, but if she stops Lilith, we might be able to stop the apocalypse." Raphael nods.

I was too guilt-stricken to fight back, able to accept my failures fully now with nowhere else to go.

"I'm going to call this one into Jesus. Please search the building." Raphael requests politely.

"Where would the barrier be emanating in this building?" I question.

"The only thing I could think of, strong enough to hold back so many demons, is prayer. A giant of faith must be actively praying to keep out the demons. If they stop praying, nothing stops Lilith from getting out or keeping those demons from getting to us." Raphael confirms.

"If I find the pastor, I will likely find Lilith." I reason.

"If you find the pastor before Lilith and he stops praying, then we are doomed," Raphael warns.

We separated once more as Raphael called for backup and rushed to protect the Head Pastor. Hopefully, I could stop Lilith before Sister Davies, or Elder Price are harmed.

Chapter Four

I took point heading off looking for the head pastor. Raphael remained in the sanctuary, praying to Jesus and reporting all that's happened. We still had a chance to stop Lilith. I should have stayed to pray as well. I already felt so guilty letting the incubus escape, and now Lilith was going to use Sister Davies for whatever Evil she had planned. Raphael says Jesus sent me, but I don't know why. As I searched the hallways, I couldn't imagine anyone else having this much trouble trying to stop Lilith.

When I failed to pray, I couldn't stop the Incubus. When I saw Lilith, I felt frozen seeing her bare flesh. My emotions consumed me as my pride consumed me with the Incubus. If I can't release my ego, I'll never be able to stop Lilith.

I fell to my knees, staring at the carpet and tears falling from my eyes as I couldn't keep going, weighed down by my emotions.

"Father God, my heart feels like it's breaking. I met a woman I liked, and I couldn't protect her from Evil. Please keep Sister Davies safe, please- please help me save her from Lilith and stop Lilith!" So I prayed, sobbing as I tried to catch my breath.

The lights all went out suddenly, leaving me in darkness. I raised my hand, creating a light illuminating my path as I reached closer toward divine energy at the end of the hall. It was a small prayer closet with a timer on the outside of it. The power felt paralyzing but welcoming as I opened the door finding a frail man on his knees praying fiercely in the tongues as if in another realm. As I walked around him, he didn't seem to notice me. I kneeled by his side, listening intently to his prayers.

"Yes, Father God, save us from this great Evil. Would you mind protecting the missionaries and the people? Look over the believers and non-believers—shield our Church. Build your kingdom here in our hearts, heavenly father. Let us not be lost to Evil tonight." He continued.

"Amen, amen, amen...." I heard from the dark corners of the room.

Lilith.

I gripped the hilt of my mace, remaining in prayer as the head pastor continued.

"I feel the darkness, father, and I feel the darkness in this room with me. Forsake me, not father. I have not- I haven't abandoned you, God." He began stumbling over his words as Lilith approached.

"Do not lose your faith now," I assure him quietly.

Lilith bloomed from the darkness in her nudity. She held a collar around Sister Davies' neck, tugging her to the ground. Lilith stood before us as we kneeled on our knees. She grinned, loving the sight.

"Heavenly Father, have I lost my soul preaching this religion? Have I disappointed you? I feel the Evil so deeply in my presence, father. Have I fallen from your grace?" The Pastor questioned himself.

"It isn't you. The Evil has arrived." I stood first standing between Lilith and the Head Pastor.

"You ready to fail this mortal as well?" Lilith tugged Sister Davies forward, making her crawl on her hands and knees.

"This is how you get off?" I mutter, unimpressed and disgusted.

Lilith held up the collar with her hand open, "She enslaves herself. The only thing more powerful than human love is their despair. A human's broken heart and disappointment overtake everything in their soul and reality. Despair is the only true way to sever a human's tie to God permanently. And you have failed her as you have failed all of humanity. As you failed your mother and wife."

"As you failed Adam and Gabriel?" I responded, standing upon a knee.

Lilith's face contorted in anger as she glared down at me.

"No response?"

"Your friend is enslaved, and you are worried about some old man who found himself a younger wife? You're low."

"Where is Adam now? Oh, he's in heaven, and you are in hell. Why?"

Lilith hisses, grabbing my throat with her sharp claws digging into my skin, "That bastard, Satan tricked me! He stole my soul and had me sent to hell! It's his fault!"

"Why did you make a deal with the devil?"

Lilith released me in shock, backing up, "How dare you? How dare you throw my marriage in my face! I have not spoken to Adam in millennia!"

"Yet you still love him." I rose, staring Lilith in the eyes.

Lilith was frozen. I took the leash from her hands, helping Sister Davies to her feet.

"Take the Head Pastor and find Raphael," I whisper.

"Thank you, Enoch."

"Don't thank me until you two are safe." I raise my mace, waiting for Lilith's response.

Lilith stood, grief-stricken as if everything had led up to this single moment in her life. Ten of thousands of years of her spirit's existence. Yet, she has never stopped coping with her marriage. I hadn't expected the words to leave my mouth, but I felt the need to clap back against her, bringing up my suicide.

"You don't know what it's like to be Satan's first pawn. He tricked the fallen angels and created demons, but nothing compares to the first, if not the reason, he overtook Earth. Adam was a sweet man. Dutiful and worked hard tilling the entire earth day after day, caring for all the animals. The entire Earth was our garden. And then Satan visited me. He was dividing us. Telling me everything I wanted to hear and everything a woman should never hear about her spouse. He turned my heart against Adam then our relationship fell apart. I had never seen Adam so hurt and angry. I meant to help him, but I turned from a beautiful wife into a tempestuous shrew. When God spoke to Adam, Adam revered it, bowed to God, and Satan told me it was a weakness to bow before God. After the first day I spent in hell, I vowed my revenge. I would outdo the devil. I took the women of this Earth. Gloria Steinman, Margaret Sanger, and many other women have brought the women of Earth to my cause. Lost for good, their families destroyed, and the fate of humanity in ruin. Only I could have done it because Satan was an Angel at the end of the day, forced to do God's will in maintaining hell. But I was an animal. A vindictive and wounded animal, making him hurt as I hurt."

I placed my hand on Lilith's shoulder. She raised her arms to strike me, but I hugged her instead. Lilith stood in shock as I embraced her. She slowly wrapped her arms around me as her shoulders fell and went to her knees. I kneeled beside her as she cried, sobbing on my shoulder over tens of thousands of years of grief, pain, and anger.

"Help me stop your army," I begged.

"I can't. I'm in too deep. I have promised too much. Earth must fall, and hell with overtake Earth." Lilith's tears dried as she stared at me with those ice-cold blue eyes.

"Father God, please cleanse Lilith's spirit of the lucifer spirit. Forgive her sins. And help her see the folly of her ways." I prayed.

Lilith shoved me away, "you... you, how dare you pray for me!?"

"I was hoping you could come to heaven with me," I admitted taking in her immeasurable beauty.

"You- you like me?" Lilith covered her mouth.

"I don't know." I hold up my hands.

"How dare you be so indecisive!?"

"Well, you're evil."

"Okay, now it's time for you to die." Lilith's tears begin trickling blood-red, falling down her cheeks down her porcelain skin.

"If we must fight. Father God be with me." I sighed, raising my mace.

Lilith made the first attack lashing out with her bloody tendrils. I had the freedom to move in such an open room versus the narrower hallway. I was dancing around her strikes getting in close enough to swing my mace with all its force. A wall of dark energy blocks my blow before she begins firing energy balls at me, forcing me to pick up my pace, dodging and hopping along, following the rhythm of her breathing for the next ball to be fired. I studied her movements, and I was soon upon her again.

I released the mace, creating a rope to lasso her, bringing her to the ground and tying her with rope laced with divine energy.

"No! No!" Lilith struggles against the rope.

"You're coming to heaven with us for questioning," I demand, digging my knee into her back.

"The way you look upon my mortal form. You should have your way with me now. You won't be allowed to have me for yourself after I get sent to purgatory."

“If I did that, I could never look Jesus in the eyes again. Besides, I’m not interested.”

“How can any man reject me? You have me at my most vulnerable. I am naked for you to do whatever you please.”

“I am an Angel, not a man.”

“You still have your parts, don’t you? The last time I checked, they didn’t turn you, angels, into eunuchs. Take your opportunity. I am offering myself to you willingly.” Lilith arched her back high in the air, her scent filling the air.

She will do anything to corrupt my soul. Am I honestly considering making love to a demon? I mean, she is beautiful. I know other angels who have had children or sex with mortals while on patrol. Would Lilith be any different?

“If you wish. I will leave you alone. We can go somewhere more private and make love until the sunrises.” Lilith suggests.

Sister Davies came to my mind. It was as if I saw Sister Davies tied up in vulnerable, causing me to stir. I had only been an angel for a few years. My human emotions and desires still felt so strong, yet this wasn’t as it seemed.

"How dare you take her form for such a perverted display. Stop at once!" I demanded.

Lilith laughed, turning back into herself, "I knew she was your weakness. I can take her form if you rather make love to that silly thing. You prefer human flesh?"

"I prefer neither! I don't want this at all."

"Oh no." Lilith squirmed away from my grip, rolling away.

"Where are you going!?" I demanded.

Lilith flapped her wings, taking flight despite being wholly bounded. She laughed hysterically, taking to the sky.

"I must thank you again, Carter. You lowered the barrier for me by awakening the Pastor. You summoned my army for me and lowered the barrier. I love you for making this so much easier by being so weak."

"Purgatory Pillar," I whispered.

"Huh?" Lilith looked down, seeing a divine halo above and below her.

As she attempted to move, heaven's light consumed her. Lilith left out a primal howl of pain as the divine energy entered her body, shining out of her mouth, eyes, nose, and ears as if the light hallowed out her spirit. Instead of being teleported, her body fell to the ground with a thud. I was surprised she was still on this plane. Usually, their soul was decided on and teleported.

Lilith began laughing as my ace in the hole proved futile.

"Hell doesn't even want me back." She laughed as tears filled her eyes, and she began to hyperventilate.

I backed up until I hit a wall a few steps behind me. I had no idea what to do with a succubus while there was an army to fight. Instead, the pillar dissolved the rope, leaving Lilith crying wildly on the floor before me. What will happen now?

Lilith was weeping on the floor, entirely consumed by her grief at realizing she faced something greater than hell or death. If you failed in the material realm and got refused entry into limbo, I have never seen someone get rejected but held but only heard rumors of God's actual punishment for failed souls. Erasure. From everyone's memory, history, and existence, to have your very soul disintegrate. I hear it's an excruciating pain from the rumors I've heard. I have never witnessed an erasure. I didn't want to see one.

We had fallen into silence as she came to grips with her fate and I contemplated witnessing someone's soul removed from existence. It didn't seem very pleasant even to consider a fellow spirit. Death, in truth, was quite a breath. Depending on how you died, natural, painful, but quick, you were left with an untouched soul. The pain falls away, and you have a new life. To no longer exist seemed impossible to imagine.

"Do you think God will erase you?" I asked quietly, finally breaking the deafening silence.

"I have committed the greatest atrocity any spirit or demon has ever fathomed. I infected every woman on Earth. I destroyed their relationships and any chance of them ever having a real relationship. All to create my demon army and have their children fight in my demon army."

"Can it be undone?" I asked.

"With erasure." She confessed.

"And that's all you can consider? I offered one of your incubi the same thing I will offer you now. You can repent. You can turn yourself to good and face judgment in heaven." I offered.

"You're so dumb. Do you know that? Not everyone wants to be an angel with no free will and no way to enjoy life's true pleasures. You all feel so lucky to be in heaven. You pretend there's nothing you desire outside of heaven."

"You believe there are things God cannot provide? Don't you realize that's why you betrayed him, to begin with, Lilith? You got it all wrong. I tasted all the things of this world: drugs, sex, violence. I hated it. In contrast, you rejoice in those things. While you cherish the ability to commit any sin, you wish without judgment or condemnation. I met a young man who was about to jump off a bridge tonight. He couldn't be more than a sophomore in high school, and one of your jezebels ruined his life. Why? So, he can go through purgatory to become some demon in your army?" I expressed from my heart.

"it's too far gone. I have already corrupted the richest and most intelligent humans. I have already given them whatever they wish to do my work. Most betrayed me for Satan. I thought I could control humanity, but centuries passed, and they only got crueler. I never expected Satan and my work would make humans evolve backward."

"You don't even care about Pablo?"

"To be honest, none of these humans are of any consequence to me. Even these little flesh monkeys they call famous, I forget their names and faces with all they do to worship Satan and me. These aren't my children. They are Adam's. Maybe Adam should have fixed his brood by killing his son Cain as Cain killed his second-born. This mess is all Adam's fault."

"Cain was your son, was he not? After he raped Eve and struck Adam, didn't he discover his mother was little more than an evil succubus? Abel was their true son, and you left Cain with Adam. Cain hated his father because he blamed his family, especially his brother, for what happened to you." Raphael spoke, entering the room. His energy filled the dark prayer closet with light.

Lilith stood, legs wobbling underneath her with barely enough energy to flap her wings as she attempted to escape.

"Cain was your seed. Adam and Eve showed your son the greatest love and mercy imaginable after his sins. That was true forgiveness and service to God because you failed. You were the serpent who tricked Eve, weren't you? Out of vengeance and bitterness. You've allowed Samael, Eve, and Adam to take the blame for all these millennia. It's time to face Heaven's Judgement. I'm taking you to see Jesus." Raphael squeezed his hand shut.

A hand of divine light grabbed Lilith before I could react. They were both gone. I was left alone on Earth for the next 20-22hrs. I don't have a watch to tell me how much time has passed since I dropped off Pablo. At least we caught Lilith. I suppose I must believe she earned whatever has come to her, but after Satan stole her entire legacy and life. The human still inside me felt she was only doing what anyone would do against their oppressor. I didn't buy either side.

Raphael was the only one who told the truth. Lilith chose what truth she wanted to say to me. I still didn't know why she did what she did to Earth or the people of Earth. Spite for her ex-lover against his children? I dealt with kids who wanted to commit suicide because their stepparents were abusive. Or the single parent was abusive or neglectful. To wait close to a million years for revenge against Satan seemed insane. To plot so much on Earth seemed crazier.

The truth she refused to tell me was that instead of seeing the Evil in Satan, she hoped she could replace him. I had never seen someone rejected from purgatory and hell. There was no hope for her in heaven either.

My cellphone began ringing, signaling another child in danger. Yet the portal didn't rip open and take me away. My phone chirped immediately after.

"Rest for a second. ETA 10 minutes." Jesus texted me.

I left, shuffling my feet back to the sanctuary collapsing in the pews, feeling exhausted down to my core.

"Carter?" Sister Davies asked in shock.

"Hey, glad you're alright." I made a brave face, straightening myself up as she approached me.

"Usual night for you?"

"Usually, I get ice cream or a hot dog, wait around on rooftops and then head back to heaven. Anything but usual. It's the strangest, hardest night I have ever gone through in my life or my afterlife."

"Your life?" Sister Davies asked as she sat next to me.

"Well, yeah, before I was an angel, I was human. A few years ago. Now, I'm on the Guardian Angel Task Force for Earth. I hope to get a more interesting planet, but I'm not complaining."

"You believe in other planets?"

"Our God is God over the solar system and the multiverse. It's not a matter of belief. It's more about acceptance of reality." I shrugged.

"How did you become an angel?"

"I don't like talking about it." I rub my elbow, looking away from her coyly.

"I didn't mean to offend you. I want to thank you, but I don't know how to thank an Angel."

"I don't need appreciation for doing my job. I'm glad you and your head priest are safe. Elder Young should be back to feeling himself a couple of days after he goes through processing in limbo, and they realize he isn't dead yet." I assure, standing up, beginning to head off.

"Can I at least pray with you before you go?" Sister Davies offers.

I was stunned by the offer. Lilith offered me sex, but this young woman offered me a prayer. They couldn't have been any more different. So I nodded politely, kneeling next to her in the pews, folding my hands, and bowing my head.

"Heavenly Father, please bless my new friend Carter. Enoch is my hero, God. When that evil woman took me to the world of death and darkness, I felt such fear and despair. I truly almost lost hope today. Carter restored my faith, and he did more than restore my faith. He made me realize how real you are, God, and how real prayer and sin are in this world. Thanks to Carter, I don't think I will ever stray from you. So please protect Carter and give him more confidence. I pray he understands we are different than the spirits and demons he must see quite often. I pray my heart can stop beating out of my chest, and we are safe tonight. Please help Carter and go easy on him because this isn't his fault. I pray my Church opens its eyes and realizes there is only God and no division or denominations. And I pray that evil woman faces justice for what she did to my friends and the poor young man she arrived with today." Sister Davies finished praying.

"Hallelujah, Amen." I closed, rising again, feeling refreshed, "did you mean it?"

"Every word." She kissed me softly on the lips.

"Wow."

"Be safe, Carter. I think you may be the only man I ever love, considering you are dead. I hope to see you in the afterlife one day."

"I pray you to find love on Earth and live your days to become an old woman with a great family. Do not waste your existence awaiting death. God wants you to celebrate life, not despair about your death. Be well, Sister."

"My name is Margaret." She blushes.

"Enoch... well, I guess I already told you. Sorry I haven't kissed since even before my death. I forgot how good they felt."

"I am sure there are many wonders you have forgotten how they've felt. I wish we could wed, and I could remind you, but- I guess I pray to meet a man like you."

"Hopefully, someone better. I didn't do too well as a husband or mortal. I must say goodbye."

"Will I ever see you again?" She asks, hoping I would say yes.

"I have no control over God's will. I am merely a servant of God Almighty and a brother to his son, Heru, Jesus the Christ." I bowed my head as the portal opened beside me.

"Goodbye, Carter." Sister Davies covered her mouth as if she were choking back tears.

The last thing I saw before leaving her was her eyes swelling with tears. I was torn through the astral portal spit out far from the Church. Yet I could still see the demon horde running through the streets. I can't spend my night worrying about Margaret or Lilith. I need to focus on stopping these demons, or there will be worse things than depressed children in counseling all night.

I wonder where this next assignment has taken me. Alright, take a deep breath, re-center yourself, Carter. There are still more humans to save before I can return to heaven.

Instead of finding a human, I met a ten-foot man with red skin wearing a trench coat. A fedora hat covered his horns. His arms crossed behind his back as he waited patiently for my arrival.

"You're my assignment?" I asked, holding my hand on my sword's hilt as I cautiously approached.

"I prayed for assistance in stopping Satan's retaliation against Lilith. Soon he will come. If the man's son returns, there will be little choice but a rapture." The demon extended its massive hand to me.

"Enoch Carter." I greet, putting my hand inside his massive paw.

"Demetri. I lost my last name after my soul was committed to hell. I have been working to stop other demons on Earth. Tonight, were more demons than ever before, and I needed help." Demetri gently squeezed my hand, then released me.

"Do you have any leads?"

"Indeed. There is one area overrun with demons. We must head to Hollywood. I believe Ahab is having a party tonight." Demetri nods.

"I've never been to Hollywood before." I smile.

Demetri sighed, shaking his head as if I could never imagine what awaited me.

Chapter Five

Demetri creates a portal bringing us into the back of a nightclub in what I imagine is West Hollywood. Even from the outside, the music was pulsating. It had a hypnotic effect making me feel at ease and anxious. I felt my wings involuntarily clicking to the beat before I noticed the man beside me looked severely different.

Instead of a ten-foot demon, I was next to a rugged man with tanned skin and a thick beard—still snug under his trench coat and fedora. Demetri gave me a nod signaling for me to enter the mortal realm from my heavenly form.

"It's for safety," Demetri assures me.

"I would feel safer with my wings."

"Would you feel safe if the entire room filled with demons who hated angels? Demons dream of raping an angel. You will not need to stay hidden for long. There is someone we must meet. If things go awry, feel free to defend yourself how you see fit. I beg of you not to ruin our cover." Demetri pleads with me at this point as we hear the voices nearing the door, clasping his hands as if praying.

I sighed, entering the mortal plane. My sword and armor were gone, but my white suit matched white loafers. Demetri smiled in approval, nudging me forward as if I owned this place as good as I looked draped in all white.

The door swung open with two gunmen carrying AK-47s wearing black sunglasses. Demetri quickly stepped in front of me, holding up his hands.

"Gentlemen, gentlemen, how are you, my friends?" Demetri said in a heavy Arabic accent he manifested with his disguise.

The two people's eyes hadn't left me, but their guns were holstered on their backs.

"Who is he?" one asks, clicking his teeth with a whistle.

"He is a good friend with your boss. We told to come to the back to skip the line and grab a meal on the way." Demetri explained, rubbing his belly.

They looked at each other. Demetri slammed their skulls together while ripping their bodies out of the doorway. With another grand slam, they fell unconscious.

"Get changed. You're already bringing too much attention." Demetri sighed as he took the man's suit and gun.

I snap my fingers, losing the suit, quickly stripping off the guard and rushing his clothes on my body. Demetri did the same, taking their socks, underwear, and undershirt and throwing them in the trashcan.

"What are you doing?" I asked, alarmed.

"If you leave them dressed, they'll feel confident to come outside. If the guards are stripped naked, they'll do whatever it takes to get home. The humans are ashamed of their flesh." Demetri notes with his thick inflection.

I nodded, learning a lot from his different approach. He stepped back inside. The kitchen was moving too quickly to notice our brisk pace inside the building. I thought he had a contact, but the way Demetri moved, he had a lead. And judging by the armed security, our meeting wasn't scheduled.

"You go first. Our lead will recognize I'm a demon." Demetri halts as we reach the center of the music. The dance floor was relatively empty.

A few people were on the floor, moving like in a trance with liquor in their cups. If you looked close enough, you could see the tiny demons and demon spores swimming in their glass, naked to the human eye. The demons sang and cheered as the humans gulped them up. The bartenders possessed husks, slinging out more demons by the bottle and pouring shot glasses of spores.

"This goes deeper and longer than I realized," I whispered.

Demetri probably couldn't hear me over the music. He seemed to be speaking, but I could hear nothing over the music. I could listen to nothing but the melody. I felt Demetri's tight grip on me as he guided me through the mind-numbing beats. I felt like I had drunk a whole cup of dirty sprite with purple in my cup. The music held a strong power over me.

"Are you alright, Carter?" Demetri asked in his normal voice right in my ear.

"Huh? Where are we?" I shook it off.

The world went back to normal as my eyes adjusted to the mortal world. I could only see a bunch of college kids and women sitting alone. The music didn't seem as loud. My heart was beating quicker and quicker until I could come to full grips with what was around me in the spiritual plane. I'm glad I listened in hindsight.

"He's up ahead, be respectful, but I think he's going to take a liking to you. Tonight doesn't have to go bad." Demetri pats my back.

"Let's get some info and get out of here." So I rubbed my eyes, beginning to come to full grips with how dizzy I felt.

We came upon the VIP area, a rosebud in the back of the dance room where a man sat in a Black Tuxedo. A wild grin on his face and a giant chandelier above his head shining a light down. His eyes met us, and his smile turned into a look of disgust. Instead of calling for security, he met us directly. Soon I was looking up to a seven-foot man who appeared human in a bespoke tuxedo. What the hell did I get myself in? What kind of trap did Demetri lead me to here!?

"Did Lilith send you here? I told you rent-a-cops if you want to stand outside and intimidate the rabble, then so be it. Get out of my club and stop harassing my honored guests." He had a delicate British accent but a sharp forked tongue.

"Who is Lilith?" I asked, shrugging.

"We are here about all the demons, wondering what happened? You make the laws, my friend. We merely wanted to show our respects." Demetri wooed.

"Lilith is the biggest thorn in my ass since- I don't think I've ever had a pain in my ass this big." So he fumed, gritting his teeth, "I didn't invite these demons on Earth if you're asking me. They are multiplying like mad and being so bold. So neither of you are human either."

"There are demons here?" I say as if I was little more than a human taking his first step into the occult.

He chuckled, thrown off guard, "Ha, I didn't say demons. Haha, this kid is funny. You, are you a human?"

Demetri revealed his proper form.

The man was shocked as he looked up at Demetri. He let out a sigh realizing it might not be worthwhile. An easy smile settled on his face as he took a seat, fanning his hands around us, inviting us to join us.

"So, what mess has Lilith got herself into now?" he asked eagerly, "Please, gentleman, join me and have a seat."

Demetri looked over to me, giving a shrug and sitting down. The place looked stunning, a modern interpretation of a royal dining room. He chuckled in absolute amusement at my wonderment. I had died too early to enjoy drinking or clubbing. This whole aspect of life was new to me. To believe so many demons spent a second life walking around Earth in a human's flesh or disguise. That's wild.

"Your friend is an absolute delight." He laughed in his British accent.

"He is a great man. So, you seem not to like Lilith much, huh?" Demetri nodded, trying to regain his attention.

"I hate that shrew. What do you want to know about Lilith?" the lead enforced.

"What has she done to unleash all these demons on earth?" I asked, stepping into their conversation and taking a seat, "Have there always been so many demons on earth?"

"Good question. I don't know which one to do first. I guess dealer's choice, so I'll pick. No, demons usually need a pass. I have been very strict about eternal damnation. Until a few decades, there had never been so much demonic activity from humans. The humans have completely submitted themselves to me and rejected my father entirely. I didn't ask. I had finally gotten everything I wanted. Yet, the humans are fickle."

"Fickle, how so?"

"Well, the principal theory I have is that humans believe in nothing. They are entirely ignorant of my father and know little more of me by proxy. For so long, everything had been considered evil or sin on Earth. Once those souls reach purgatory, they never reach hell. Until recently. A few men had died then after that hell has been overflowing."

"Who was killed?"

"Oh, this is decades before your time, kid. JFK, his brother, MLK, and a wise man by X. were All killed. No one asked. No one cared. And then so many souls have walked through hell since. Humans stopped caring for one another. So I stopped caring for anything good. I can't count the men who asked where their money was or asked to see who their money went to but cared nothing about who came to their funeral or how their spouse or kids had done. So it's a bit sickening, honestly." So he continued, happy to discuss his perspective.

"Who are you?" I finally asked.

He grinned, wagging a finger at me, "haha, I will answer that when you tell me what you are doing with a demon detective."

"You first."

"I am Lucifer, thee Samael."

"Samael, that's the name of a former archangel, the angel with musical powers?" I asked.

"I was a glorified choir director. I aspired for much more, but my father would have none of it. Wait. No one knows how did you- who are you, sir?" he pressures with his eyes.

"Sammy, how about you pay attention over here. My friend got lost in the music and liquor. I need a lead on Lilith's underbosses, Ahab and Jezebel. Where are they?" Demetri enforces.

Lucifer clicked his tongue, eyeing Demetri over before returning his attention to me. His eyes begged the question as his mouth fixed to answer Demetri. I remained silent. My heartbeat knew if I revealed myself, I would be in the fight for my life. Demetri controlled the situation, clicking his tongue as if trying to get a cat's attention.

Lucifer sighed, looking over Demetri, "You think you're a pretty big guy, huh? Dare to compare?"

"I'm not here for you, Sammy. We don't want to interrupt your party. There's a giant demon horde on Earth. Whether or not you know, it isn't my problem. However, it'll be a real shame if all your patrons died by a horde or are raptured away."

"That does sound quite bad for business. You believe there's a real horde?" Lucifer laughed.

Demetri didn't smile or frown. His face grew stern, releasing a moment of sullen mourning as he let out an exhausted sigh.

Lucifer laughed harder, "I assure you, gentlemen, you can relax. Lilith talks a big game, but those three are all secure. There has never been an actual demon invasion. Not since the Medieval Age and once again in the dark ages. The demons got purged, and the evil spirits returned to hell, where I securely reign supreme."

Why would I worry myself? If the Devil himself didn't believe there was a real threat? First, though, Demetri was perturbed.

"You're a fool. The biggest fool I had ever met in my life. You are here sitting on Earth beneath yourself. In a weaker form playing barmaid to look cool for some college mortals. Hell is in shambles. The darkest, most vile souls have not only escaped hell but have devasted hell and now are on Earth. Those three, Lilith, Ahab, and Jezebel, have not only escaped hell but have been present on Earth planning their takeover for decades. That guy was the first to see the horde and how it grows. They have been reproducing by spores. Look around your club, Sammy! Or have you been pretending to be human so long you lost sight? You can't even see how your club falls apart around you, lost in drugs and money. You have completely lost grip of hell, and the mortals who worship you on Earth have forsaken you for Ahab and Jezebel while Lilith pulled strings. Come on, Carter, this washed-up SOB is no Dark Lord. We must find the new Dark Lords to stop this invasion because our buddy Sammy can't be bothered." Demetri asserted, standing up to leave.

"I am Carter, Enoch Carter, an ethereal detective. I faced off with Lilith tonight. I got trapped inside a church surrounded by at least ten thousand demons. Demetri came here because he thought it would help, but I guess you are more Lucifer than Samael these days. Lilith is in Heaven now-

"Heaven!? What- How did she-

Lucifer fumed, gritting his teeth and tossing a couch out of the VIP, rolling out into the carpeted floors. Demetri and I hopped back, unsure if a fight were to ensue. Instead, he fell to his knees, looking out on the dance floor to see our suspicions were confirmed.

"Dad isn't going to let me hear the end of this one. I had one freaking job to keep my kingdom." Lucifer roared louder than the music itself for a moment before the beats took over once more.

"What is going on, Sammy?" Demetri inquires, grabbing his AK-47 as the room gets alarmed by Lucifer's sudden mood change.

"It's not what's going on. It's what has happened, you idiot. Angels weren't entirely perfect, and I was proof of that. God, he is the only perfect. When a third of the angels followed me, Heaven was destabilized and had to restructure itself. Likewise, when the first humans failed to obey God. With or without my intervention. Albeit if humanity failed, then I would inherit Earth. A son's recompense for failing his father. All I had to do was direct all the evil souls to hell and keep them out of Heaven and off Earth. So, I created a few kookie religions to make agreeable humans sensible and weed out the troublemakers. His creation was clever. And every time my father intervened, either I was to pay or humanity. It's much easier to get humans to blame themselves than to face erasure."

"You created religion?" I gasped, surprised.

"Well… no and yes. Man creates religion, and God created man. I send in a man under my possession and keep close eyes on these prophets. Sometimes their wife or trusted advisor. Then when God's prophet meets an unexpected end. My people can takeover because they infiltrated at the very beginning. However, I didn't imagine what would happen from dividing so many humans for so long. They blame each other, but it's my followers and me. It's not exactly grounds for erasure. Subverting humanity and leaving them with the problems is sort of my thing."

"Like when you and your angel buddies thought it would be fun to mate with humans and other mortals, creating this entire problem." Demetri snorted.

"Well, what can I say? I'm the freaking devil." Lucifer smiled, picking himself up.

"This one you can't blame on humanity. You failed at your job. You're getting erased." Demetri said unforgivingly.

"I didn't open any of these demon portals. I gave no one any demon spores. And I never would have let those three wounded souls out of eternal damnation. I don't even know Ahab, never seen him before either. And Jezebel and Lilith are two old flames unable to let go of a grudge. Eve wasn't so bitter. Some people can't handle good-loving, you know Enoch? You met Lilith. What man could keep his hands off her, you know?" Lucifer attempted to gain my sympathy.

"I sent Lilith to Heaven for erasure with Archangel Raphael. I refused her today. Not before she told me how she ended up in hell and who was responsible. You admit to sleeping with Eve too?"

"Ha, you think you can pull some sting operation on me with only the two of you?" Lucifer shook his head.

"I'm only here to end the demon invasion. I could care less about your sex life. There are far more attractive women than Lilith.

Maybe your lack of discipline got you in this situation." I accused.

"You were supposed to be the cool one, Enoch! Low blow, mate!" Lucifer held his heart.

"Tell us how to stop the demon invasion?"

"A shit ton of guns, a shit ton of holy water, a fucking rapture, and maybe an army. What the hell did you listen to yourself? What would you tell me if I held you captive in your establishment and asked how to stop an Angel Invasion?" he eyeballed me closer, studying me for the first time since we met and finally taking me seriously.

"You almost got me, but I see your point," I noted, realizing the severity of the situation, and there was no solution, at least not one my enemy would tell me.

"Now, if you gentlemen would like to be murdered but first viciously tortured and mutilated for my enjoyment before returning to your pathetic afterlives as someone's dead pet dog. Bugger off before I lose my bloody mind and kick you out myself." Lucifer snarled, standing up and flexing his muscles at us, clenching his teeth so hard his veins popped out of his neck.

"Were you sleeping with Lilith, so you didn't realize she was betraying you the entire time without even liking you?" So I deduced how easily Lilith offered herself to me while on duty to get out of the arrest.

Lucifer stared at me, gritting his teeth and letting out a deep breath as his shoulders slumped and his head bowed. He grew quiet, lighting a cigarette and sitting back down. Then, as he exhaled, he looked at his hand, noticing the demon spores covering his packet of cigarettes before putting it out. He held his head, rubbing his temples as if nursing a migraine.

"I thought we were in love, honestly. I had never met someone so evil. I loved her. I believed her when she told me she forgave me." So he wiped away a tear.

"She offered herself to me to get out of her arrest. I do understand why you fell for her, but you couldn't see through her act at all?"

"Can we focus on the invasion?" Demetri demanded.

"Lilith is in Heaven under lock and key, held for questioning. You tell your bosses you want to testify against her and report she's entirely to blame. Her forces will back down without their leader. Then you send in the army to kill off the stranglers. I sincerely doubt those three could pull off a full invasion under my watch."

"When is the last time you have left Earth actually to spend time monitoring hell?" Demetri sucked his teeth.

"I visited for about 12 years-

"That's like a weekend vacation for someone with your lifespan. What year was that even?" Demetri fumed in rage.

"Well, after the dark ages, I had to get out of there, man. With the Bubonic plague, everyone became an idiot, and no one trusted my authority figures. I knew nothing, said nothing, and stayed in hell until the Africans came to save Europe. I bet father had to plan centuries to fix my screw-ups." Lucifer smiled with a bit of laughter in his voice.

"There's going to be a rapture because of you! Your incompetence and greed have caused the end of the world." Demetri screamed at Lucifer, pleading with the being to listen and process what he had done.

"Huh, I guess it did. Well, I imagine that was how it was always meant to be, after all.

There are better planets than Earth out there. Maybe you could spend the last few decades of humanity's existence cultivating a new planet like Earth. There is a different sun and about five light-years away by Blackhole with a 25% chance of surviving the Blackhole. For space, those are good odds!" Lucifer mocks us.

"Rapture?" someone overheard our conversation.

"Rapture? There's going to be a rapture!?" someone else began talking none too far away.

"So many innocent souls will die because of you, Sam! I was on probation! I could have been an angel, and millions of other demons won't make it! You're not snaking your way out of this to pretend you had been in hell the whole time. You're going down, Sammy!" Demetri bellowed out.

Lucifer smiled, welcoming Demetri to attack him.

"Send us to purgatory and kill us if you get the chance. I'm going to hold him down. If I get a good grip on him, don't let him escape." Demetri gave me little choice before he wrestled with Lucifer.

I felt time itself slow down. There was pandemonium on one side of the club as the demons in the room began panicking about a rapture. The human bodies they possessed began rushing around the room, seeking an exit. In front of me, Demetri had been fighting with the Lord of Evil after telling me to stay hidden.

I could use one pillar to purgatory and send them both to erasure right now. There was no doubt both souls would get judged and sent to hell. However, the pillar worked slightly differently than the prism. The prism sent people to intake processing at purgatory. My pillar ability sent people straight to the fiery pits to burn away their human and ethereal connection leaving most spirits. The spirits survive the fiery pits until erased. Suppose they don't escape right from under Satan's eyes because he's too busy destroying Earth to hold dominion over hell. I see how easy it must have been for Lilith.

"Father God, please guide me and help me not to make things worse." So I prayed, lifting my hands.

I looked at my human hands and black suit, realizing I blended into the crowd perfectly. Demetri had the upper hand on

Satan. Satan merely laughed at him, knowing he could change his form or slip away using blood magic as Lilith had done. I learned a lot from my fight with Lilith. More from my meeting here.

"Demetri, let's get out of here. The place is starting to riot." I shout.

"What? I have him! Kill us both!" Demetri screams, pinning Satan down by the throat and bashing his head into the floor.

Satan was battered and bloodied, his eyes egging Demetri to give in to his evil nature as a demon and commit himself to eternal damnation.

"Demetri, think about your probation! I met a reformed Demon today! You can get reformed as well! Commit yourself to Jesus and help us instead of serving him. He represents all your lesser desires. He represents everything keeping you in that demon form. Reject him. If you accept Jesus, I assure you of salvation."

"Nothing can save you! We had so much fun. Come on, kill your friend Enoch! Let me feel your power after you hid it this whole time!" Lucifer goaded us on to give in to our every temptation.

"I accept Christ as my savior." Demetri relented, raising his hands as he backed away from the fight.

The club patrons split into one group running out of the club for their dear lives. And another group possessed by demons beginning to destroy everything around them. Regardless of their groupings, the rioting was exiting out into the streets, and you could hear it stirring with the humans and other demons outside the club. We were trapped.

Lucifer began stirring. We stood none too far from the growing destruction inside the club—a fire grew from the DJ booth and a second at the bar.

As human patrons attempted grabbing the liquor bottles from the bar, a few fell into the flames screaming in agony but running away on fire for safety. But, regardless of the destruction, one man driven by a spirit of greed had been grabbing bottles. Then, as one bottle of vodka fell into the flames, I lost sight of the man in a cloud of smoke as the fire rose. The rioters began building a fire with chairs and furniture, and a few had been pulling the DJ from his booth into the bar's flames.

I had no idea how I would escape. If I blew my cover, I might fly out, but it was too narrow and the ceilings too low. So I would give away my identity and then fight a group of pissed-off demons.

I turned to my side to see Demetri back in his disguise. We began jogging for the door in human form. I looked over my shoulder to see the pissed-off demons had faced off with Lucifer. Then, as The Dark Lord tried to calm them down, they each pounced on him at once, holding him down to the best of their ability. Then, after successfully getting him down, he transformed into an Archdemon form. Then, with horns and wings, his skin turned a pale red. He gored one of the demons through the chest, killing it instantly. After seeing The Devil transform. The others turned into their demon forms. Though the Devil broke through the ceiling, he was soon tackled and beaten by ten-foot and twenty-foot demons directed by vengeful spirits. We didn't have time to stay and watch the fight.

However, I did see a large demon chop-block Satan behind the knees, then two others grabbed his horns, holding him down. Four demons finally saw their eternal tormentor on his knees and took the opportunity to punish him—giving him their hardest hits all at once while two twenty-foot demons held Satan down by his horns. More minor demons had been punching him and stomping on him, getting their hits in, until two spirits came and entered Lucifer's vessel. The demons holding him by the horns ended up ripping them off from their sheer strength. Lucifer screamed in agony loud enough to hear from outside the club. The last thing I saw was his horns ripped off and him turning back into human form. I did not see the demons and spirits stop their attack on his weaker vessel.

I had been running with Demetri as we ran, seeking cover as the demons rioting in the street due to the talk of a rapture began overturning cars and seeking more fires. Throwing whatever they found into storefronts and through apartment lobbies—harassing anyone they found with an empty vessel to occupy. While some humans did join in, most looked on in horror as their greatest nightmares had come true.

If Lilith hadn't overthrown Satan before, then it's confirmed now. She had outwitted the Devil and sat pretty in Heaven, likely refusing to cooperate. I had more than half a night until I could return to Heaven. And I can't leave this place worse than I found out as badly as I want to go back to give a mission briefing to Jesus and strategize a better way to handle things. There will be no convincing him out of rapture if I tell him the same thing I heard from Lucifer.

I need to get to the bottom of how to save these people from the invasion. If not, many humans will die, and demons will never be allowed into Heaven. So we regrouped in an alleyway a mile away from Satan's West Hollywood Nightclub.

I haven't had any contact with the only two people involved at all will be Jezebel and Ahab. But, for better or worse, they will want to know Satan is down. I had no leads and no way where to find them.

I need to gather my thoughts. I have no idea where to go next from here. And the screams of the demon rioters grew by the passing seconds of us catching our breath. So we peeked out to see Satan's head paraded around the streets.

Please, God, there must be a way to stop these demons and evil spirits.

Chapter Six

I was exhausted, my clothes drenched with sweat weighing down my movements. My arms were weary as I had spent the past three hours with Demetri. My sword of the spirit and his Gatling laser gun. We had both tapped deep into our reserves. I don't know how much we had left. Fighting off a hundred thousand demons and dark spirits coming to us in waves—sometimes overwhelming us entirely, forcing us to run and hide in a new location before being hunted down only minutes or seconds later. Enough to take a deep breath, say a quick prayer, and continue the assail against darkness. There is absolutely no way out. At this point, it only feels like I am taking down as many before my erasure from existence.

"Carter, I hate to tell you this, bud." Demetri began as his laser suddenly stopped firing.

"They don't tell me and just fix it!" So we shift positions as I take point defending him from a bumrush of five lesser demons.

"I have no solution, Carter. I'm out of micro fusion cells. We need a plan and quick." Demetri finalized.

"Heavenly Father, please help me. I don't want to be gang-raped by a hundred thousand demons." So I cried, feeling my weakness consume me entirely.

I felt a hand grab me by my collar as we both fall to the ground. A trick Demetri had used once or twice before, judging by how Demetri held his chest. Teleporting took a lot from him, what we had learned the first time as other demons had the same ability. We knew the second time that it gave us the most time to recover, around five to ten minutes instead of a few seconds before they rounded the corner or found us in an alley.

We were in some temple, empty, dark, and dilapidated beyond repair. I could hear nothing for miles away.

"Where are we?"

"I don't know. I didn't think it through. I thought of what you said in the club, giving my spirit to Christ. I didn't fully have control over myself. So I grabbed you, and the portal took me." Demetri explained.

"We're not alone," I whisper, feeling new demonic energy watching us.

A buzzing noise loomed over our heads as I saw the wisps hovering overhead. I held my breath. My heart froze as they circled faster and faster until a loud buzzing noise blew out my eardrums. Demetri shook his head, hearing the roars and howls from afar growing closer. I squeezed Demetri, finally entering my complete angel form and taking him to the ethereal plane where we hopefully could see what we were fighting.

The wisps were a raging red spirit, a blue rotund sloth spirit, and a voluptuous lust spirit. They fled in three different directions when they saw us enter the ethereal realm. We had no real options and nowhere to run.

I peered out of the temple windows to see demons approaching on all sides, a mile of monsters of all sizes carrying weapons.

"Whoopsie!" A shrill voice cackled behind us.

We both turned our heads to find a bug-eyed imp carrying matches. It lit the kindling until the flames burned down its fingers, then giggled again.

"Whoopsie!" cackling out of pure enjoyment.

As Demetri cornered the imp, the imp defecated an inky, oily substance with a diarrhea stench.

Demetri's eye's bulged as the imp's bug-eyed swirled in his socket.

"Whoopsie!" the imp lit another match, setting itself ablaze, emptying its intestines to create a massive explosion.

The blast threw me through the window. I opened my eyes to find the ruined wooden church burning as black smoke filled the air. Demetri busted through the wall set ablaze. He was screeching and yelling until he could drop to the ground, rolling until the flames had burned off his clothing. Demetri picked himself up and soon fell back to his knees as he saw the army approaching us.

Demetri patted my back. I nodded as we accepted our fate. We might take a few down, but it was over. Sadly, not even an angel and a badass demon can end this invasion alone.

"I am sorry for failing you twice in one night, Jesus. I'm sorry I couldn't return to heaven to see you again, my brother. I love you, Christ. Please, don't forget me." So I prayed, fighting the tears in my eyes as I lifted my blade.

"Let us die fighting." Demetri asserted.

"If we can take down as many as possible. It'll at least make the next team's job easier." So I sighed, holding out my hand and summoning a halberd.

I swung my staff with a giant heaven's steel ax. Able to slice through demons like butter. It would at least make my job easier.

The first demons broke their line of scrimmage. Then hundreds more pursued until the demons wholly overrun us. I sliced through the monsters. I was lifting them in the air and tossing them off of me. I chopped off their heads. Took the legs off the giant ogres and the more prominent thugs to bring them down to size—finally, taking its head off with a well-placed strike to their large jugular veins.

Their numbers were endless. As one demon distracted me, another chop blocked me behind the leg, taking me down, soon punches and stomps by enough feet to call it a parade. I limped to my feet only to be tackled back to the ground. I lost sight of Demetri but could hear his screams of utter pain as they attempted to rip off his horns.

From the sky, I saw a beam of light. A prominent figure clad in heavy knight's armor. Two strong wings with a 10ft wingspan carried down an absolute juggernaut of a man. The violence stopped as the demons paused, looking on in awe at the magnificent spectacle as justice lowered from the heavens. I had only heard myths about the legendary warrior angel—the one who fought Lucifer one-on-one and broke Sam's neck.

Archangel Michael landed with an earth-shaking thud. He was clasping back his wings and unsheathing his flaming greatsword, holding it effortlessly in a single hand, lifting a shield in the other, unburdened by the sheer size and weight of either.

"In Jesus' Name, I am the one who God sends to end blights. Surrender now or prepare for your erasure." Michael's graveled voice bellows out his last and only warning.

The demons had paused entirely and were murmuring amongst each other, seeking one of them brave enough to take on Michael first.

The ground began to shake as a lumbering, scaled, fire-breathing Arch Demon sauntered up to Michael, releasing its flames upon him as it shapeshifted into a dragon. The Arch Demon struck as the ground around Michael began to disintegrate into nothingness. Michael spun on the balls of his feet. Michael's blade followed, cleaving into the Arch Demon.

The Arch Demon immediately spread its dragon-like wings taking flight into the sky. Michael's blade held all his weight until it began slicing through the demon's hide, leaving Michael on the ground as the Arch Demon flew, its blood splattering down upon us as it attempted to regroup.

"Almighty God, Almighty Buster!" Archangel Michael's prayer booms like lightning as he charges a particle beam in his hands and then releases the divine light into the Arch Demon's flames as it dove onto Michael.

Michael, with extraordinary grace, dodges the Arch Demon's reptilian head as it attempts to snatch him up in his jaws. His great ethereal sword came down in lightspeed, hacking off the demon's head before its body could finish reacting. The Archdemon's blood sprayed from its neck. Michael turned, already charging into the army of demons.

As they attempted to run, he raised a wall of divine light, trapping us all inside. He proceeded to slash through the demons. Each swing of his sword takes out five or ten with his vorpal waves projecting from each swing. If the blade didn't kill them, then the divine energy took down another twenty. Michael moved as if the armor was weightless. Yet when he landed or moved too quickly, the entire battlefield shook.

As I gathered myself, regaining my composure somewhat to find the hundreds of thousands of demons all dead.

Archangel Michael lifted his helmet, revealing a man with charcoal skin, fiery eyes, and a short black buzzcut. He marched up to me, extending his massive, armored hand.

"You are Enoch?" he sounded surprised.

"The same. Thank you for saving me."

"Jesus has saved you. I am merely his instrument." Michael bowed, saluting me across his chest before standing tall again, "I see I forgot one demon."

Demetri was bleeding, battered with his bones and horns are broken, and saw Michael, not even bothering to fight back, bowing his head for his suffering to end.

"Demetri, are you alive?" I called out.

"Not for long, my friend. You must take up the trail alone now." Demetri raised his hands high.

Michael moved without either of us stopping him and lifting Demetri with one hand despite his massive size. Michael held him up as he could easily rip him in half. He drops Demetri, tossing him aside like trash as he looks on to find the smoke trail of another demon horde approaching.

"You two need to heal up quickly. Will be a long night of battle." Archangel Michael sheathed his great sword, dismissing his shield to the ether.

"They, they broke me and used me like a whore. My kind. I- I cannot fight." Demetri is broken and bloodied.

Michael casts away his sword and shield for a giant spear decorated with inscribed scrolls sealed with divine magic. Michael looked me in the eyes as he drove the spear with enough force to drive through Demetri's chest. I bowed my head, having seen more extraordinary brutality to know when one needs saving from their misery. Demetri gripped the spear, trying his best to keep himself alive. Michael smiled using only a single hand as his other hand had already been preparing a spell above him.

"I wash over you in the blood of the lamb Jesus Christ. I release you of all legal bindings and demonic contracts. I sever all soul ties and spiritual debts. I wash you clean in the blood of the lamb. I end your life you bring you anew as a warrior for Christ." Archangel Michael recited.

"The divine intercession," I whispered in awe at the true power of the simple prayer of war.

Demetri's body rose from the spear as the scrolls grew, wrapping around his body, fully sealing him. Michael grabbed the spear like a handle for the cocoon radiating with divine light.

"What did you do to him?" I asked in shock.

"I prayed for him." Michael dully offered, beginning to march ahead.

"Where are we going?"

"You want to fight the demon horde and watch over your friend simultaneously?" He asked me, abruptly stopping and staring me dead in the eyes.

"Uhh- sorry."

"Enough talk and questions. After a few minutes, it'll be ready. For now, we- you see, this is why you make sure you have fully killed a demon." Michael tossed the cocoon aside as the Archdemon began to rise.

Michael was defenseless, cursing himself for using his weapon to heal Demetri. I looked down at my sword stepping between Michael and the Archdemon. I've never fought an enemy so strong before in my life. Or my afterlife.

In a split second, his tail whipped out, sending me flying. My wings caught the sky, carrying me afloat before I could go too far. I beat my wings quicker and quicker. The Archdemon had me in its sights, releasing fireballs causing me to swerve, tossing myself side to side. Why did it have to be flying?

Chapter Seven

The Dragon was the most brutal fight I ever had. Trying to fly while defending myself from the fire felt impossible. All my focus went to trying to fly straight, leaving me little mental space to protect myself. The best I could do was avoid taking real damage while being unable or too afraid to fly in to land any real damage.

I fly higher into the sky above the Archdemon, giving me more time to think and process a plan rather than wasting more energy.

I cast away my sword, "Father God, please help me defeat this beast and bring peace back to earth!"

A bow and arrow appeared in my hands, a large bow created from Alderwood from the forests of heaven and the arrows made of angel steel. I was always a horrible flyer, but I got my highest marks in archery and firearms in Guardian Angel training.

I felt my power returning to me, my will for victory. I soared higher in the sky as the Archdemon chased after me. I flew high enough to where the oxygen thinned out. I turned, firing an assault of arrows as quickly as my arm could load, piercing the beast's wings, throat, and eyes. The Archdemon smacked against the ground with an earth-shattering boom.

I remained in the air, knowing it wasn't over, but at least I had slowed him down.

"Michael, go!" I shouted.

Michael resisted for a moment, but he was unarmed, and we could both hear the demon horde coming to protect one of their generals. Michael relented the retreat but grabbed Demetri's cocoon and set off, spreading his wings and flying away.

Only seconds later, the Archdemon was surrounded, dead. The demons screamed and cried out in pain over their fallen leader. I didn't have anything in my tank to fight these demons. I could hear the roars from distant archdemons falling upon my location.

I raised my hands in the air, "I wash over California in the lamb's blood."

Thunder clapped in the background. The clouds joined together as lightning pulsated through their shadows. I lowered my hands, and the clouds broke, blood raining down. Demons cried in agony as the blood melted their faces down to bones. Several monsters had turned back into humans, shocked at their transformation. All those beyond saving were attempting to escape the rain but couldn't get far. The Archdemon itself has been melted to nothing as the storm picked up, its clouds covering all of California.

I flew off in Michael's direction, weary and exhausted as I could observe how the rain subdued most of the demons. They were on a rooftop none too far away. Michael applauded me as I landed next to him.

"Bravo! Raphael had told me you were a clever one. A former human as well, quite interesting indeed. I believe you may have contained California, but we are getting global reports all over the earth. We could try pleading the blood over the entire planet but-

He shook his head, denying its viability as a genuine option. Instead, he sat down on the ledge, looking over the demons transforming back into a human or being melted alive.

"A rapture would be a much less painful way. The blood is corrosive to any nonbeliever." Michael mentioned.

"Out of the millions of thoughts running down my head at once-

"I am not criticizing you. I didn't believe it was a true blight, but the battle turned into day and blackened into night. Their numbers were endless. Even I tired. Raphael had warned me, but I didn't believe him."

"Warned you?"

"You were with him, you are Enoch."

"Well yeah. That's my name." I laughed.

Michael opened his mouth but said, "Do you remember your life on earth?"

"Somewhat. I remember wanting to leave, ha. I remember wanting things to be over, but I don't remember too many details."

"I have never been human. I hear humans go through it because they had died too long to remember naturally. Their minds would have otherwise gone to dementia or insanity rather than attempt to perceive today's world and their past life."

"What are you trying to say, Michael?"

"Our leader Metatron had gone missing about twenty years ago. Now. You are here." Michael notes.

I hadn't even considered such a thing possible.

"But I was human. I was an actual human. I didn't live thousands of years ago. I'm from Jersey!" I defend myself.

"Yeah, but sometimes human spirits are reincarnated. Some believe it's a reward, but Jesus teaches us it's to hone a sword for God. Look, I'm not saying you are him. I guess it was my way of complimenting you. You fought an Archdemon. Only Archangels have such power." Michael nodded.

"I didn't necessarily overpower it."

"You outsmarted it. Quite honestly, it's far more impressive. I would have just cut its head off. You played at its arrogance, then shot it down to use its weight against it. I'm impressed. Are you ready to head back to heaven?" Michael asked as the sun rose over the horizon.

"I have ten more hours left on earth, and I intend to use them. I have to find Jezebel and Ahab."

"Two people out of so many humans. I can never tell them apart, only that they're not demons. I wouldn't waste your time. Unless you want to be responsible for pouring the lamb's blood over the entire planet, there is no ending the blight. There has never been a demon invasion so big. So many humans had given their souls to Samael. Now, Sam is dead. I knew if Sam had died, there would be a rapture. He meant too much to God. The only one he ever loved more was Yeshua. It hurt God so deeply when Samael betrayed him. Yet, we all knew it was inevitable."

"How was it inevitable?"

"We are all born for a purpose Enoch. Big or small. We all play a role in God's design. Sam wasn't satisfied with God's design, yet he came to earth to do the same thing. He fled his responsibility in heaven, and he fled his responsibility in hell. A few thousand years later, Jesus came to earth only for God to see if the men were truly evil or if there was good worth preserving."

"Well?"

"Jesus was killed by the evil that governs only men. Humanity isn't evil, but humanity fails to see the evil in these god-kings ruling over them. So, slowly the entire planet erodes into evil. But, as Jesus puts it, the humans are good-natured but have never seen goodness in their existence." Michael explained before yawning.

Michael looked down below, then up high. Though he aligned with my beliefs, I was still sifting through his words to process my perspective. I never saw humans as evil. But, though, I saw great evil in society. So I guess the sheep are not to blame for following wolves disguised as shepherds.

"How does Jesus still defend the humans after they killed him?" I finally asked.

"Jesus forgives. God does not. The Adonai tore Rome and Greece asunder. He ruined the empires and slave nations and brought them all to ruin. Jesus exposed the evil in the so-called religious cults damning the name of God and separating people from salvation. There is no religion. There is only a relationship with God. Yet, they killed Jesus, and the church remains unfixed and corrupted."

"Hence all the reformed demons as pastors?"

Archangel Michael nodded, taking a labored breath, "the war against evil seems endless. We aren't gaining the upper hand. More death and more humans are born; a decade later, there are more demons. Humans are born and deny God, virtue, and hate one another. It made the war endless when there was once peace."

"Can we end it?"

"I believe the rapture is the only way. Samael was the last person defending the sin on earth. Without him and these demons, there is only one way to save humanity."

"What about the Divine Intercession?"

"You need a team of angels to prepare the ritual over the earth. It will not spare the evil of bloodshed and suffering."

"Will it protect the innocent?"

Michael rubbed his chin, "I have never seen a Divine Intercession performed on more than one person at a time. You would need an army of angels praying at once to perform the prayer."

"How many?"

"At least one thousand. I am pretty sure most would want to go through with the rapture. We have all lost friends and family fighting this scourge. I would lend my help, but if you fall one angel short of one thousand, I am helping the rapture."

"When I get back to heaven, I'll start asking more angels," I confirm.

"I pray you are successful. It'll be a relief to use a non-lethal method to quell the blight. How about I leave my weapon with you, and you hand me yours? You may want to remain on earth, but I do not." Michael nodded back to Demetri's cocoon.

I nodded, holding out my bow as it transformed into a basic longsword. Michael held up my blade to the sun, tilting it slightly and extending it to create a great sword through his will. He seemed satisfied with my weapon's purple hue rather than his red tint. Without a goodbye, Michael gave a stiff gust of wind to thrust him into the sky. He was soon out of vision flying back to heaven the long way. I suppose it was an option for me as well if I could fly long enough.

I felt exhausted. I only had half a day before I could return to heaven. I will find a safe space to wait for Demetri's Intercession to end. I was only glad Michael had spared his life.

Chapter Eight

I found myself back at the Mormon temple. The demons were all dispensed, yet the barrier remained. I stepped inside, holding Demetri on my back, grounded by his massive weight. Michael made carrying him look effortless. He felt like my cross. Caught in the mess, I started—one of the few trying to end the blight or the rapture. I stopped at the steps and wondered why I had returned here. Both sides of good and evil seemed bottomless, unforgiving, and inhumane. No matter what, one will never know if they pleased God. Even Angels quake at the chance to appease God yet never truly know. These demons spent their lifetimes worshipping Samael. All for them to turn against him and kill him in his club. There seemed no end to evil or good. I wonder what awaits beyond good and evil?

After so much death and bloodshed in God's name, I had nothing left inside my soul but a yearning for peace. There had to be a way to stop either side from gaining victory. I didn't know it.

"Enoch, you've returned." Elder Young was wearing a white smock and a straw hat, holding a garden hose.

"Hey, I apologize for sending you to purgatory. I wasn't expecting what I saw." I bowed my head.

"All is forgiven by Jesus our savior, my young friend. It gave me time to think and reflect on how far I had come. I spent so much time living as this human. I had almost forgotten I was a demon. I dearly wanted to but was unable to forget." He began but shut his mouth quickly.

"You seem humbler than when we met."

"I was so close to descending into hell. I felt my very soul run cold." He shivered under the 90-degree sun.

"I came back for wisdom, I need a way to stop the rapture."

"The rapture is a catholic figment."

I shook my head, having no time for his deceptions, "I need to speak to Elder Price."

Elder Young nodded his head, giving a gesture to head inside.

"I pray you to have peace in your new life."

"What are you carrying? I must ask. The item seems so fascinating. The angel's technology is truly beyond our times." His fingers trailed the wrappings.

I set the casting upright, displaying the demon seals and divine inscriptions.

"So, the rapture is real?"

I nodded quietly, unable to disappoint another person.

"I would ask God for mercy, but I'm too embarrassed at my foolishness. I must ask you to forgive my rudeness, my friend. I came out here to forget all about these things for a time. So please go about your business without my involvement." He waved me off.

"Wait. I have one question. How does one become a reformed demon?"

He looked insulted, but as his eyes looked over the scrolls again, he began to piece things together, "What in God's name does an angel have a concern with a demon?"

"My friend was badly injured. The only option was to use a prayer known as the Divine Intercession. It secured him for now. However, the spell will end soon. I want to be able to help him on the other side."

"The Divine Intercession. One of the strongest prayers a mere mortal could utter. The Jabez Prayer and Divine Intercession could change a human's soul from evil to good. So, this is angel technology?"

We both looked behind us to see Elder Price with Sister Davies close by his side, helping him stand as his cane kept him steady. He was palming the scrolls. The scrolls began to hum to his touch. Then, tightening its wrapping, he ran his fingers along with the golden handles and the angel steel stave binding it together.

"My friend was a fellow detective. Last night, we were with each other when we witnessed a local club owner killed by his clientele. It's been a very rough night. We were hunted by them all night." I wiped my eye, trying to cope with the guilt building up inside me, swallowing my tears.

"My spirit tells me you became an angel trying to hold all your grief within you. You learned how to be strong. As a child, you learn to be strong, but we are all still soft as a child. You are strong, but your heart did not harden to the world like everyone else's. Your strength came from remaining soft." Elder Price pats my back.

"Gee, thanks." I rolled my eyes.

Elder Price chuckled, "Ha, I do not mean soft like a rabbit or a deer. I mean, your heart is soft. Your blood is warm. You didn't allow the world to turn you into another one of the cynics. I see in your eyes you're a dreamer. You believe in the vision in your head. You didn't want to live in this world, but how do you enjoy living in the next?"

"Not much better, quite honestly. There are angels from so many different species and planets. Finding human angels is quite difficult. Life is lonely, but I get by." I admit.

"You astonish me. I have lived for so long, yet you are the one living in the afterlife. I never imagined an angel so young."

"I was twenty when I died."

"Twenty? A baby in truth." Elder Price welcomed me to follow him.

"We were about to sit down for lunch. Would you like to join us, Enoch?" Sister Davies asks me.

"If I'm welcome." I lifted Demetri on my back.

"Of course, you may join us!" Elder Price gets a firm grip on my forearm.

I carried Demetri on my right shoulder while Elder Price steadied himself on my left arm as we walked into the Temple.

"Last night was the most horrific night of my life. I do not remember losing faith to such a degree in fifty years." Elder Price let out a dreadful breath.

"I agree. I had never been through so much hardship as an Angel. Things must have gotten worse."

"Things have always been bad. We are only beginning to see the aftereffects of generations of curses, sin, and distance from God. We cannot save the saved. We cannot save the kids who grew up in church. It's the people outside God's reach that need help."

"There is no one outside of God's reach."

"Yet they remain untouched and lost." Elder Price gave me a stern look.

I zipped my lip, letting him go on his train of thought.

"I saw them last night. The monsters are running rampant. I have seen them for a year now but never so many. We remained to hide in here for our lives when it's the lives outside of the church that need Jesus." Elder Price gripped my shoulder.

"If I don't find Jezebel and Lilith, then there will be no one inside or outside the church. The earth will either be absorbed into a full blight or God's rapture."

"Yes, but we have known this for thousands of years. Have we not known of the threats of good and evil? Of God's wrath and Satan's trickery? People are so lost in fear of God or of the government. That's what created all those wayward souls in those monstrous bodies. What of beatitudes? Do we not come to others speaking of the mercy and love of Jesus instead of the judgment and wrath? I believe if we hadn't persecuted those souls and condemned them to their fates, perhaps there would be no good or evil. There will be us skinless apes chasing fabrics and rocks as our ancestors had done. Why not be more than our ancestors? Shouldn't we want to be more than a skinless ape with guns and opposable thumbs? Is true divinity not the ability to love the people around us vulnerable and daring as if jumping off a cliff? Have we grown so far apart that we must sacrifice our lives for damnation we have known since the first man and woman came to existence? So, the future will fall to atrophy, bravo, and beautiful. Our gift is the present. So, one day God will destroy us all, or evil will destroy us all. Until that day, what type of life do we live? What kind of relationships do we have with our neighbors? We have thousands of minutes or hours until our eternal damnation by an Almighty God. Did he not at least give us a beautiful life while we breathed in our lungs? Have we become so forsaken-?

"I think I might know where Ahab is these days, at least where he spends a lot of time." Elder Young relents cutting off Elder Price.

I shook myself away, lost in Elder Price's rant of focusing on the blessings of life rather than our blunders. I had almost fallen asleep in my sandwich and soup prepared by Sister Davies, who sat to my left.

"I was not done." Elder Price protests.

"Elder Price, I thought your sermon was beautiful, but I believe Enoch needs real answers." Sister Davies patted my knee.

"These are the real answers! The Beatitudes are the answer!" Elder Price retorts fiercely.

I rubbed my chin but had no idea what he mentioned. The Beatitudes were not in my guardian angel training. Or whatever he had said. So I scratched my head, trying to place it in my memory banks, but I had never heard the word in my life.

"The promises of God." Elder Young catches on to my confusion.

"Oh crap, you're right! Wait, God promised never to destroy the earth again! He couldn't possibly bring about the rapture."

"God did not bring the rapture. When John projected his revelations, The Anti-Christ brought the apocalypse. Then Jesus returns. Jesus' return doesn't bring about the rapture or the end. It's his antithesis." Sister Davies schools me.

"So, in other words, the Kingdom of Heaven is defenseless due to the promises?"

"Not exactly. I believe Elder Price's point was so much time has been wasted on condemning sin. And none of it has been used to enjoy the miracles and blessings of our lives."

So Sister Davies says before sipping her soup while it's still hot.

She had Campbell's tomato soup while Elder Price shared a can of chicken noodle soup. Elder Young had Progresso clam chowder. Elder Young scowled at me as I looked over at his bowl while he seasoned it with salt and pepper. I averted my eyes, my view falling back upon Sister Davies and her bright smile as she studied me.

"Do you get to report all this back to heaven?"

"To Jesus himself." I smile at her intrigue.

"You have met thee, Jesus Christ?"

"He's my boss. He's our King."

"Your eyes were so intense when you said that. I love your conviction."

"Too bad you two can't get married." Elder Price chuckled.

Sister Davies blushed, looking down at her lap, nibbling her sandwich.

"Stranger things have happened," I smirked, considering the idea.

"You would need a baptism first, but we can have you two wed by evening." Elder Price pushes.

"Oh my God, this is not happening." She mutters, covering her face with her hands.

"Ha, cheer up!"

"Elder Price, please stop teasing me. Enoch would want nothing with some silly girl like me."

"I happen to like silly girls." I smile.

Her eyes finally met mine as her smiles returned with two flustered cheeks. I lifted her head, kissing her forehead.

"Alas, I am dead."

"I don't care."

"Really?"

"I am to be chaste regardless. I will rather be married to an angel." She confirms.

"I am interested, but I need to pray on this. Seriously it's a lot all at once." So I held my head feeling my night compounding on my body and spirit.

"I did not mean to add another stress to your life. I know young love when I see it. You are here for a reason. Please take your time. Feel free to reheat your food. We have beds as well where you can lay down and rest. You are safe here." Elder Price bows his head.

"Thank you for your hospitality. I don't remember the last time I sat down to have a family meal like this one. Thank you all." I clasped my hands, wishing I had a way to repay them.

I headed to the sanctuary feeling a different connection to this Temple after fighting to defend it and being graciously welcomed. However, the marriage proposal was a bit weird. I tried marriage. It's an excellent technology but not my cup of tea. At least not in my situation. Everyone's love life is different. Maybe if we had gone to therapy, I would have lived. I try not to live in the past. The future was before me.

My phone rang, alerting me of another case. Already?

No, it was a phone call.

"Hello?" I asked, unfamiliar with the number.

"You're not back yet."

Lilith?

"How did you get my number? You're supposed to be in detainment."

"I am in detainment. You are supposed to be here as well! Now, where are you, I asked?"

"I don't answer you!"

"Look, you were my phone call. I had one. The ops gave me your number. I need you to tell them the truth."

"I don't know the truth."

"You're the only one who knows the truth. I know you were there when Samael died. They think it was a hit! I refused to speak until I talked to you."

"I'm a detective, not a lawyer."

"All the lawyers here are angels Enoch! They want me to burn for what I did. And now that Lucifer is dead, I wanted him overthrown and finally punished. Well, I'm not too sad he's dead, but I didn't do it."

"It was a riot in the club. They heard about the rapture before I could get any real intel. He wasn't too fond of you."

"Who are these days? Well, maybe you, my offer still stands. I need you to get to heaven now!"

"Hopefully, a few more hours in a jail cell will mellow you out. I spent an entire night fighting demons you let onto the earth! I nearly died or worse because of you. Do you think I'm going to help you? Those demons wouldn't have been there if it wasn't for you."

The line went quiet. I took a deep breath, weaning in the dead silence. Should I hang up and leave Lilith to rot?

She coughs as if I was supposed to speak.

"Well?" She asks.

"Well, what?"

"I will be yours if you help me. If you choose to have me erased, then so be it. I am yours if you choose to do what any red-blooded man would enjoy. Suppose I am to serve you for eternity, then whatever. I will not let these hypocrites judge me. You will be my judge."

"Does Jesus agree to those terms?"

"You need another man's permission?" She sucks her teeth.

"I need to know this will not compromise the Kingdom of Heaven." I retort.

"Enoch, you have my permission. When you return to heaven, please me in the grove. I will talk to you directly after you have reunited with your friend." A third voice answered my concern. A soothing yet stern voice like a father's trying to calm his child in a tantrum.

"After?"

"Lilith has been here for hours refusing to speak. She is refusing to move. She just keeps repeating your name. So, please figure things out. I do not know anything of an agreement you two have previously made nor any relations you have had. However, she seems intent on hissing her forked tongue in your ear."

"He's testing you, Enoch." Lilith teases before the line cuts.

I rubbed my temples as my teeth ground against each other. I tried to breathe but couldn't find the air. I was in such pain down to my core. How did I become her last lifeline? How dare she ask such a thing from me before my King!? And his voice. He sounded like he didn't even know me anymore. After this night, I didn't recognize myself either.

I wanted to pray but couldn't open my mouth.

Sister Davies had been standing over my shoulder, having heard the entire conversation standing in awe. We didn't say anything as she helped me stand to my feet from the shock, processing everything going on momentarily as if life was moving in slow motion. So I got led to the dormitories on the upper level. She sat on my bed, hoping I would join her for a few minutes, but I felt too vulnerable, and the temptation felt too great. So I turned my back to it all, passing up the issues heading to the windows and closing curtains to sit in the pitch black.

I lay there trying not to cry from the overwhelming emotions pouring over me. I felt delicate hands rubbing my back and the stubs of my wings left when they got concealed. It took everything in me not to stop the massage because it was the only thing keeping me together.

All I wanted was to figure out why so many of us humans were committing suicide. I tried to put an end to their senseless deaths. I have been fighting for my life because of some feud hundreds of thousands of years before birth. My problems weren't adding. They were multiplying exponentially.

I must stop the rapture if I can do nothing else but stop God from pulling the trigger on earth. Maybe Lilith is genuinely the only person to help me achieve it. After I wake up, it's straight back to heaven.

Chapter Nine

Suppose I could describe Heaven to a mortal. It's light. When you first see Heaven, it's blinding light burning your eyes. As your eyes adjust, you see streets paved with golden bricks connecting to a metropolis floating above the multiverse. Fields and forests, mountains, and beaches. Every natural wonder is unpolluted and without litter. The air was always fresh and breathable, giving every breath its aroma rather than the smell of sewage or manure habituated to the senses.

I have been told everyone sees something different once they leave the city. I had my mansion and farm stretching a few acres—a blip in the entire span of how grand Heaven is over the whole multiverse and all possible lifeforms. Heaven doesn't reign over a single solar system or universe. All life resides underneath the Kingdom of Heaven. There was more than enough space for any person who died. Instead, you can go days or acres without seeing another person at times. When people get lonely, they head to the city for events or get an occupation. Some people spent their eternity taking vacations around Heaven. Everything was free and provided for by God.

I enjoyed coming through the gates. You never know if you'll meet someone you know or once met. I have seen old teachers and family members around. You would think it would be sad, but it feels more like a reunion. Sadly, the line was longer than I'd seen before, and I recognized no one. Different species, lifeforms, and spirits awaited their turn with St. Peter, who never had time for anyone or anything. At least he enjoyed his job.

"Enoch!" St. Peter called out to me.

Just when you thought you knew a guy.

"Enoch, you are going to speak with Jesus, correct?" he asked as I tried walking past him.

"I am to speak with a prisoner first."

"There are no prisoners on my list for at least 25-50 years from now. And judging by this line, I will not be able to see them from another one hundred. So what is happening on Earth?" St. Peter asked.

"Hey, I'm next! I've waited ten years to reach the front of the line!" A red-skinned alien with four arms and an insectoid head complained.

"Then you can wait a few minutes, so I can have a conversation, Gozer Gurzak. It's not too late to go to Hell. Patience is a virtue. Remember that Gurzak." St. Peter fired back at the alien.

"Whatever." Gozer crossed his arms, huffing under his breath.

"There is a Blight on Earth. Demons have taken over the entire planet at this point. The majority of humans are possessed or under demonic influence. If not yet, their leaders are hired by Jezebel and Ahab. It looks like a rapture." I explained, rubbing the back of my neck.

"As I presumed by the length of this line. So, as I was saying, you're speaking with Jesus? Let him know I need help up here. It's getting ghetto, like a Walmart with only one register open. My Heaven is becoming a personal hell. I need a vacation, and I need help. What is purgatory doing?"

"Uh... I don't know. I haven't checked purgatory yet. I'm just getting back from Earth."

"Earth? You were down there during a Blight!?" St. Peter covered his chest.

"Ha, yes, I was, but I grew up during The Blight. The worst part was that we didn't realize the Blight was already happening. When I was down there, a single spirit could erupt into spores. I had never noticed it, but you could see the spores on the people, their food, their liquor, and inside them. So the demons and evil spirits have a special relationship with humanity. I don't think an Angel and human could ever fully have that bond as a former human." I admitted.

"Why? You're an Angel and a Human." Gozer asks.

"Humans aren't very bright. When we work hard, we only do it for money or recognition. Demons prey on that and use it for their deeds. The Evil Spirits exploit it and use it to reproduce. Humans are breeding grounds for demons. I wondered why human life was so difficult and why it was set up the way it was arranged. Now, I get it because demons and Lucifer created it. They ruined it. And there's one woman who tried to stop it." So I bowed my head thinking about Lilith.

"You think you can fix it?" Gozer asks me.

"Why do you care?" St. Peter sighed.

" I don't, but I hate to hear such a thing happening to someone's home planet. I am here because the Zulaks invaded my planet. They killed all the men and children. I died before I saw what they did to the women. We fought, but they went planet to planet doing the same. I hate to hear what happened to our planet happening to your planet."

"You think the demons are our Zulaks?" I asked, curious about his perspective.

"I don't know about that exactly. In a way, yes, I think they are your Zulaks. Demons go universe to universe, planet to planet, corrupting us and making us do evil to one another. We had no answer. I hope you find one for humanity." Gozer extends his fist to me.

I nodded, giving him a fist bump, giving dap is universal.

St. Peter smiled but held back his words, letting us both through the gates to continue his work. Gozer looked around in wonderment, chuckling as he sprouted transparent veiny wings heading off on his way.

I enjoyed taking the streets though I guess practicing flying would be better.

I had a lot on my mind and decided to walk to the precinct where I knew Lilith and Jesus were waiting. I imagine this is how Adam felt coming between those two. So I moved a mile in a few minutes. So even though I wanted to take my time, I couldn't help how fast I moved.

"Hey Carter, how's it flying?" McDowell, the receptionist on duty, is operating the front door.

"Feels pretty horrible, man. There's a blight on the earth." So I frowned, unable to keep up my guard.

"Hey, don't blame yourself, man. It's Lucifer's fault. All this is his fault, so don't beat yourself over it." Raphael hugged me.

"Glad you're alright!"

"Me? Enoch, I thought I lost you. Michael told me you decided to stay on Earth. What we came across wasn't even the smallest of it. We have lost Europe and Southeast Asia entirely. The East and west coasts of the USA are gone. The Midwest is posting a fight, but they can only hold out so long." Raphael briefed me.

"How about Africa?"

"Northern and South Africa are under siege, but the terrain seems to be holding off a full invasion," Raphael reported.

"Latin America?"

"Surprisingly untouched. The Catholics have released their Jesuits to fight the demons and train young men and women to become spiritual warriors. If we can replicate their tactics, we might be able to win the war." Michael joined us, shaking the hallway with each step.

"Glad you're alright, Michael."

"Likewise. So, this still hasn't hatched yet?" Michael rubbed his chin.

"I guess not."

"Then here, take your Angel Blade back. I'll take this to Uriel to see why it's not done." Michael extended a switchblade to me.

"What is this, Michael?"

"You must speak to the witch. You must end this, Enoch." Michael presses the blade into my pocket and then snatches Demeteri's cocoon.

"You know there's another way."

"You know you must look Jesus in the eyes after all this is done. There's a special patrol going to Hell to maintain order. You let that succubus live, and I guarantee I will drag you down to Hell to ensure you're in the legion." Michael stopped and stared down at me.

I took my blade and created a single coin.

"Heads or tails, Michael?" I asked.

"I'm not playing your stupid game." He scoffs.

"I'll call it. Tails." I flipped the coin in his face sidestepping him and tripping him to the ground catching Demetri in the process.

Michael lifted himself to his knee, clenched his fist, but stood his ground, "You will choose Lilith over Heaven?"

"I will choose the truth over continuing the comforting lie." I extend my hand, helping him up to his feet.

Michael crossed his arms behind his back, staring at the sky in contemplation before asking his next question, "You truly don't see she is manipulating you?"

"Michael, I don't even know Lilith! I have never spoken to her before today. I want her dead as much as you do if you saw what I saw today. She started this Blight, and she can end it! If we kill her, we ruin any opportunity of stopping the rapture!"

"Why would you want to stop the rapture? To say such a thing is sinful." Raphael asked me.

"If I truly believed Earth and humans were beyond saving, I would say let it be done. Today I met a boy who had never met Christ. His life was in shambles. And the Hell he lived in made him believe there was no heaven. If we make the gates so narrow, no one can get through, and then all those humans will be committed to Hell or an eternity in purgatory when they could be on Earth becoming better people. I was human. I know we're not perfect, but God. If I have to go to Hell to stop this with you two, then let's go. However, if she has a way to stop this that requires sparing her life, she has already committed her life to me. And I will drag her to Hell with us to clean this mess."

"We'll need more than the three of us if we were to go to hell." Michael patted my shoulder.

"With Demetri and Lilith maybe, we can survive," I suggest.

"You have too much faith in the forces of hell." Raphael frowned.

"Why are you both second-guessing me?" I snap at them.

Michael and Raphael looked away from me, staring at the ground and around the room but avoiding eye contact with me.

"Where is Adam?" I bark for their attention.

"He's praying in his cave. He's been there for the past century attempting to attain enlightenment with Siddhartha." Raphael informed.

"Can you please get him? One of you? Putting those two in the same room together would solve our problems. We still need to get Ahab and Jezebel." So I rattled off, unsure if I was honestly being heard.

Michael's face wore worry and mistrust over it as if I had betrayed him. His fiery eyes studied me with great intensity. I stepped back as if I had been punched in the face. Michael sighed, walking off without another word, sheathing his weapon as he went on his way.

"If Michael is out, then I'm sorry. I must stick with the will of the Sephirot." Raphael hugged me and then left me standing alone.

I sighed, feeling as if I was the only one who knew the truth. Why this all started and why we were at war with Hell. They treated Lucifer as if he were still an angel. But, as if he is innocent in all this, it was never Lilith's fault now, was it? Why was she trying to reclaim Earth? Not from God, and she never asked for a war with Heaven. She wanted to take Earth back from Satan after losing it to him in the first place. Lilith wasn't fighting to destroy Earth, only to destroy Satan's grip over it.

Satan lived on Earth as its king. He watched it fall to ruin and profited off the destruction while Lilith rotted in Hell for over a hundred thousand years. In my eyes, she's served her time. Satan was probably back in Hell, preparing his defense and trying to reclaim order.

I fear we lose our only chance at stopping Lucifer for good if we kill Lilith. I have an idea, but I know no one is going to like me for it. And I'll likely be sent to Hell for even suggesting it. So, I won't recommend it. I won't tell anybody. I know how to free Lilith and end this war for good.

I was walking down the hallway, moments away from my destiny. Every step felt so heavy and labored. As if I could turn around, spread my wings, and fly away from this moment forever. Instead, I kept walking closer to the interrogation rooms as if walking waist-deep in a swamp. I was arriving at room seven and taking a deep breath before entering.

Lilith was sitting, restrained in a straitjacket, and chained to the floor. Her lips had chapped, her make-up ran down her eyes in tears, and her eyes were half-open as she stared at the ground.

"About time you got here." She spoke first.

"I'm going to make this quick, Lilith." I sighed, drawing my weapon.

Lilith smiled unimpressed as she nodded, accepting her fate without question, "I was hoping for you at least saw some good in me."

"I saw what you chose to show me."

"Stare me in the eyes when you do it. Let me know you have some balls." Lilith growled at me as the betrayal drove her to rage.

I stand before she holds my sword while wrapping her hair around my hand, holding her head to watch me as I stab her in the chest. I drove the blade deep into her and twisted it. I gripped her head as life began fleeing from her body.

"I wash over you in the blood of the lamb Jesus Christ. I release you of all legal bindings and demonic contracts. I sever all soul ties and spiritual debts. I wash you clean in the blood of the lamb. I end your life you bring you anew as a warrior for Christ." I recite the Divine Intercession, returning her soul to Christ.

Lilith's body began to glow a radiant light as my sword expanded, wrapping around her in a silk cocoon. Pink ribbons and velveteen taffeta decorate her shell. Then, waving a hand over it, I could feel the power radiating inside as the prayer held her inside as her spirit attempted to fight back. It wasn't long until the cocoon went silent.

I sat by the cocoon, wondering what people would say about putting myself in this situation so close to the hell expedition. It might have bought me some time, but there was no fighting the inevitable. I felt better knowing there was a chance to end things peacefully but knew I would pay a higher cost in the respect and trust of the sephirot for trying to save Lilith.

My phone rang with a text message from Jesus, "It is time."

⍰

Meeting Jesus was never easy to go through. I approached a man who is indeed holier than thou yet still humble, making the entire process very self-reflective. Jesus didn't like meeting in the office or at his home. Instead, I walked through the mountains, hiking down to a wide-open valley where my Lord and savior sat alone looking into the waters. When he felt my energy, he turned with a bright smile waving for me to join him.

"You have traveled far to see me, my friend. Please come down." Jesus cheered me on as I came down the last kilo to him.

He laughed, ushering me to a seat and pointing to the cocoon on my back.

"You always keep me guessing, Enoch." Jesus chuckled.

"Thank you, Jesus."

"What made you use the Divine Intercession?" he asked.

"I felt like it wouldn't have fixed what she did if I killed her. I thought she at least needed to have a chance to atone before she is erased."

"Yes, that's nice, but why did you do it?"

"She was too beautiful to be forgotten." I bowed my head.

"Do you love her?"

"I felt sorry for her and all she has lost. I felt connected because I'm a human-like she was or is; however, that works, I don't know. But, I felt like she was fighting for humanity to regain what it's lost to Lucifer. I didn't feel her war was with Heaven or Earth. I think she got what she wanted with Samael being dead or back in Hell."

"He is gone." Jesus nodded to confirm.

"I saw, but I didn't believe he would truly be lost."

"Death is final. In contrast, you have a special take given your duties. You do understand; you are dead and gone from the mortal world. You serve The Kingdom of Heaven. The interests of humanity have far diverged from obeying Heaven's Will. Hell is under the jurisdiction of Heaven. And Satan was meant to keep it from ruin. Do you understand the conflict of interest in keeping her alive?" Jesus got very stern with me.

"I did."

Jesus sighed with relief, patting me on the back, "Oh, thank God. I thought you had no idea. So, it truly was an act of love. Ha, I knew you had a soft spot in your heart left. Do you wish to marry her?"

"If I may, when this is all said and done, if things are fixed, and if she accepts."

"You understand you are dead from marrying a woman just like Lilith. My concern is that you haven't learned anything in life or death. So you go about performing your duties. You tell me what you think I want to hear, but you're dishonest to yourself." Jesus frowned in disappointment.

"I am in lust with Lilith. She offered me her body, and while I resisted at the moment, it's something I craved so deeply and missed more than anything else on Earth. And she has it and wants to give it to me."

"Yes, but to ignore her sin, the evil she has done, and to bring you to her side. First, though, you used the Divine Intercession. There might perhaps be a chance you brought her to your side."

"I meant to bring her to the Kingdom of Heaven."

Jesus smiled, hugging me tight, "That's why I am proud of you. Despite all she had done and all the evil she committed. You saw the light of God inside her soul."

"Thank you, Master."

"You taught me something, Enoch. Pull yourself together. Geez, you don't have to cry." So Jesus pushed me off, brushing himself off.

I wiped my eyes as Jesus walked to the waters.

"I was married once. I had a child. She was not as devoted as I. When I left home, telling her I was following God. She thought I was crazy. Abandoning them, but she came from a well-off family. Not very religious. I didn't imagine when I left. I would be crucified. I didn't know things would turn into all that's before me. I was a man, Enoch. Like yourself. God brought me to where I am today. Yet, your compassion for that woman you're carrying. It's beyond anything I had seen. I don't believe you're in lust. I think you fell in love."

I rubbed my neck, knocking my hand against the goldenrod holding her altogether. I recoiled my hand, quickly realizing Jesus was right. I still had contempt in my heart for her actions, but at its core, I wanted to protect her more than my duties at this point.

"I want you to return home and rest. You two will both be on the expedition to Hell. Ahab and Jezebel have taken Lucifer's place in Heaven and on Earth. Bring justice to humanity by giving them the same fate as Samael. Those two are to be erased no matter." Jesus confirms, folding his hands behind his back as he takes his proper form.

His frail frame filled with muscles. His auburn-brown hair aged rapidly into long thin grey strands swiping at his ankles. His face grew shrewd, darkening as his beard fell to his naval. He was developing a few inches as he stared at the waters.

"I have maintained my form for so long, to be recognized and immortalized but for naught. People remember my image before my death. They do not remember anything I have said or done. I will join you in bringing justice and will fight alongside you."

I was stunned by the severity worn on his face and posture. It was not a pacifist. It was a man born in chaotic times and under a lawless world controlled by corrupts. An innocent man was murdered for attempting to fight back against the evils of the world. He turned to me. His eyes had a fire that made me bow my head, unable to face him in this form.

"I have held my hand for centuries. Refusing to punish humanity for its sins because I believed they would choose virtue. Yet, they are controlled by the vilest spirits on Earth. I need you to know. You cannot stop the rapture, and you cannot save every single evil soul with this prayer. I was idealistic, and I didn't know how truly evil Earth would become. My death has allowed the greatest atrocities to be done in my name by the same people who killed me. What has been done cannot be undone. They indoctrinate their children, enslave their most capable people, and use schmucks to manipulate and manage the rest. I will join you in Hell because if this mission does not work. I am ending it all." Jesus assured me, extending his hand.

"I understand."

"Look at me when I'm speaking to you." He demanded.

I raised my head, staring at his face. Despite his form and fire, I saw the same compassion and love in his eyes.

"We can save a good number, but we cannot save them all. I need you to understand. Humans individually choose their fate. My father nor I have any say. Humans choose to go to Heaven or Hell, and no one forces them. When we eventually return to Earth, I need you to understand it. And after we have walked through Hell together, you will understand why it must be so. So I will go to protect you all. To ensure our victory before directing our army to Earth. Are you with me, Enoch?"

"Always, my King, I will fight by your side."

"And I will fight by yours." Jesus lifted my chin, patting my shoulder and giving me a smile like a concerned grandfather.

"What is it, My King?"

"Your compassion will be your undoing. Lilith will fail you. She will betray us the first chance she gets. And I fear even then. You will not hold her accountable for her actions." Jesus squeezes me tight.

"I believe she'll be grateful. I don't think she is fully aligned under good but-

"I am not asking you what you think. I am telling you Lilith is going to betray you." Jesus releases me, unleashing his wings and hovering above me.

I stood beneath him as he took flight, leaving me in the field with Lilith. I sat where he sat, looking down at the waters following the creek. I saw my face, but I didn't recognize myself anymore. I had memories but felt there was more to my life I couldn't uncover.

Damn, I need to lay down.

Made in the USA
Middletown, DE
31 December 2022